A Father's Kisses

Also by Bruce Jay Friedman

Novels

STERN
A MOTHER'S KISSES
THE DICK
ABOUT HARRY TOWNS
TOKYO WOES
THE CURRENT CLIMATE

Non-fiction

THE LONELY GUY'S BOOK OF LIFE
THE SLIGHTLY OLDER GUY

Plays

SCUBA DUBA
STEAMBATH
HAVE YOU SPOKEN TO ANY JEWS LATELY?

Screenplays

SPLASH!
STIR CRAZY
DR. DETROIT

Collections

FAR FROM THE CITY OF CLASS
BLACK ANGELS
LET'S HEAR IT FOR A BEAUTIFUL GUY
BLACK HUMOR
THE COLLECTED SHORT FICTION OF BRUCE JAY FRIEDMAN

A Father's Kisses

A NOVEL BY

Bruce Jay Friedman

DONALD I. FINE BOOKS

New York

Donald I. Fine Books
Published by the Penguin Group
Penguin Books USA Inc., 375 Hudson Street,
New York, New York 10014, U.S.A.
Penguin Books Ltd, 27 Wrights Lane,
London W8 5TZ, England
Penguin Books Australia Ltd, Ringwood,
Victoria, Australia
Penguin Books Canada Ltd, 10 Alcorn Avenue,
Toronto, Ontario, Canada M4V 3B2
Penguin Books (N.Z.) Ltd, 182–190 Wairau Road,
Auckland 10, New Zealand

Penguin Books Ltd, Registered Offices:
Harmondsworth, Middlesex, England

First American edition

Published in 1996 by Donald I. Fine Books
an imprint of Penguin Books USA Inc.

3 5 7 9 10 8 6 4 2

ISBN 1-55611-499-0
CIP data available

This book is printed on acid-free paper.
∞
Printed in the United States of America

For Patricia J. O'Donohue

Prologue

*C*OULD *I, WILLIAM H. BINNY, take the life of another individual? When my own existence was not at stake? And my loved ones were not in peril? Could I commit such an act when I was far from the field of battle where I once had the honor of serving our nation? Cut down a fellow human being whose hopes and fears and dreams were similar to mine? Not only for him or herself but for a better America?*

Could I look such an individual in the eye—and not slip up from behind in a cowardly manner? Or carry out the deed from some protected enclave—or even worse, in anonymity?

If such a situation arose, would I be up to the task?

These concerns were the furthest thing from my mind when I first encountered Valentine Peabody.

Little did I realize how soon it would be before I was forced to grapple with them.

Chapter One

I FIRST BECAME aware of Peabody while I was enjoying my usual breakfast at the Edward Bivens Diner, a small, noisy establishment that is not particularly outstanding in its decor, even by diner standards. There are a dozen counter seats, half that many booths and some framed and grease-stained pictures of past governors on the wall, each one a grave and self-important-looking fellow with mutton chop whiskers. Breakfast is what you might expect—juice, eggs, sausage and the like—but the price is a good one—$1.69—and it has gone unvaried for as far back as I can remember. (The bagel, which has caught fire in our community, can be substituted for toast at a small extra charge.)

The owner, Ed Bivens, is a tall, taciturn fellow who can usually be caught standing behind the counter, tucking the flap of his shirt back into his pants and staring off in the distance as if his mind is on large issues. His wife, Betty, a short, squat feisty Nicaraguan woman operates the grill as her private domain. When the shack in which she was living with her cousins burned to the ground, it was Ed, as the leader of our First Response Team, who had resuscitated her (and also pulled her mattress out of the flames). And thus had begun their romance, Ed having no idea of what a little pepper pot she would turn out to be.

The diner is situated directly across the road from the statehouse and the customers, for the most part, are statehouse regulars with an occasional feed salesman thrown in. A favorite topic of discussion is the local councilman, who went off to Washington to take a post in the new administration—and the fat government contracts he was supposed to throw our way. Thus far, he had not thrown any, and the feeling was that he had gotten caught up in the Beltway social scene and forgotten where he came from. He himself had written home to say that

7

being close to all that power was like a drug. We took comfort in knowing that eventually he would have to return home, drugged or not, and face the music.

I CANNOT PINPOINT exactly when it was that Peabody made his first appearance at the diner and proceeded to turn my life upside down. I do recall that it was at a particularly bumpy period for me. In a short space of time, I had lost my wife and been thrown out of poultry distribution.

It was the former circumstance that caused me to lose my bearings. From the moment I first laid eyes on Glo at the hog auction (and watched her wriggle with delight during the baby goat sell-off) to the day she closed her eyes for good, I do not recall our exchanging a single cross word. She was taken by Mary's Lung, an affliction thought previously to affect only the wives of nineteenth-century Welsh coal miners. But Glo had come up with it. Had I known that she would be snatched away from me with such cruel prematurity, I would have treasured our eight years together all the more. I cursed myself for teasing her on occasion about the weight she had put on, as if a few extra pounds—thirty or forty to be fair about it—could affect the essence of a loved one. It can't—and her rare and genial good nature prevailed to the last. As the end drew near, she told me not to fret.

"We'll be together in the afterlife, Binns. And I'll be a slim-bones."

I clung to that possibility—and had it not been for my concern for our daughter's well-being, I would have made immediate preparations to join my departed wife—no matter how much she weighed.

If there were happy prospects in view at that time, I was not aware of them. Still, I thought it best to keep up a pretense of structure in my life, lest it fall apart completely.

Each morning I would drive my daughter to the middle

school in my pickup and wait to make sure she had gotten safely past the cluster of boys who had begun to take notice of her charms. Though she had just turned eleven, Lettie was tall and long-legged and had developed what the school nurse referred to as "breast buds." I was not personally fond of this phrase, but there was no question she had them and could easily have passed for fourteen. (The nurse had alerted me that her "menses" would be coming along shortly, another term that I found unsettling. Had she merely pointed out that Lettie would be getting her period, I might have received the news with more equanimity.)

Many of the boys in the schoolyard were of Hispanic origin, a surprising number of South Americans having settled in our midst. Though I try to be open-minded about this development (*we* like it here, why shouldn't they?), it is no secret that their offspring tend to be more hot-eyed than our own. (Their own scholars might even admit to that. And who knows, perhaps it has something to do with their proximity to the equator.) Whatever the case, Lettie, fortunately, did not have any idea of the effect she threw off. She did not wiggle her hips or flounce around in the style of her more precocious friends. Nor did she take the Cindy Crawfords of this world as her role models. If anything, she was a duck-walker. Yet who knows, she might, unwittingly, have been some kind of Reverse Flirt, her very modesty serving to inflame the smoldering (and perhaps innocent) Latinos. So I did not feel secure until I saw her safely past that group and on her way to her first class.

Only then would I begin my day, such as it was—which consisted of polishing off one of Ed's substantial breakfasts while I perused our local newspaper. On occasion, one of the statehouse regulars would leave behind his Wall Street *Journal,* and I would give that esteemed publication a riffle as well, although, in truth, the world of derivatives and debenture bonds is a mystery to me, and I had no portfolio to protect.

Still, business is a part of our world, and I felt I should at least try to stay abreast of it.

After ingesting the day's news, I would linger for a bit and ruminate on where I had gone wrong; inevitably, my thoughts returned to the day I had told my supervisor at the poultry distributor that I needed to take two months off to find myself. Though all but a week of it was accumulated vacation days, my supervisor was unhappy nonetheless.

"We're jammed up," said Mr. Wittels. "Can't you find yourself in the office?"

"I tried that and didn't get anywhere."

"Suit yourself," he said, and walked away without further comment.

As it happened, the decision turned out to be one of the biggest mistakes of my life. Two months later, not only had I failed to find myself, but when I tried to get my old job back I found that it had been filled by Toni Wittels, my supervisor's wife, a registered nurse who had been coaxed out of retirement, and was having the time of her life, sitting at my old desk and dreaming up new routes. Having tasted the heady and fast-paced world of poultry distribution, Toni was not about to return to a humdrum existence. (And who could blame her?)

Where I got the feeling that my job would be waiting for me upon my return is something I cannot explain. Certainly I had received no such assurance from my supervisor. Yet had I known the result of my decision, I doubt that I would have behaved differently. The time was valuable in that I got to read the works of Mr. Henry Makepeace Thackeray, our own Ralph Waldo Emerson, M. André Gide, Chekhov the Russian and the tragedies of the Bard. (I did not get to the comedies—they are on my list—but I did knock off several Molieres and a Corneille.) To my delight, I discovered that the great Edward Gibbon was understandable to someone such as myself—and that the ancient Romans had problems similar to ours—such as where were they going to get the money for bridges.

I also wolfed down *Candide* in one bite and found it intriguing that of all the author's mighty works, only that fast-paced little ninety-pager survives.

One might argue that I could have digested these works while continuing to work in poultry distribution, but I feel that I could not have done so full-out.

AND THEN ALL of a sudden, just as I was settling into a dark future, there was Peabody, as if by sleight of hand, taking his seat at the counter, pretending to be one of us. Which is not to say that he succeeded. *He* may have thought he did, but he didn't.

What set him apart—from my point of view—was his mode of dress, which ran so contrary to our community style. He wore soft olive-colored slacks, moccasins with a tassel on them and sweater coats of a variety that are not purchaseable at our local stores. (And that would include the new mall.) Then there was his shoulder purse. Say what you will about us, we are not the shoulder-purse type.

He kept the sleeves of his sweater coats rolled up to his sharp elbows, in an effort, I would guess, to look like an everyday person, but it didn't work. He still stood out. Tall and slender, he had shoulders that were stooped and rounded in the manner of a distance runner. A shock of reddish-brown hair fell forward on his forehead, which I envied on sight, since my own hair has thinned out considerably. (Though I dislike the style in others, I had taken to wearing it in a modified comb-over, using ultrahold hair spray to keep it in place.) His mouth was open a good deal of the time as if he was astonished at everything he saw, and he had a tendency to pant expectantly, like a big dog, anticipating a treat. (You almost expected a couple of paws to come out.) From time to time, a droplet would form at the end of his sharp nose, which he would erase with a discreet swipe of his sweater sleeve. That was his single departure from an overall sophisticated style.

11

He took what appeared to be an inordinate interest in Ed (they seemed to have a past connection) and the diner—which puzzled me since Ed, his detached style notwithstanding, never struck me as being all that fascinating. If anything, it was Betty who claimed to have descended from high-born Nicaraguan stock (temporarily down on their luck) who was the more fascinating of the pair. (Granted, Ed does have the excellent collection of mouse figurines.)

As to the diner, it may not be a greasy spoon, but it is certainly not to be confused with Le Cirque Restaurant in New York City.

Yet Peabody would marvel at it, craning his long neck around from time to time and saying: "You've got quite a place here, Ed."

Then he would take an appraising look at Betty in her housecoat and bedroom slippers and say: "Did you know that you're a beautiful woman, Betty?" a comment that even Betty must have known was a reach. She is a hot little package who certainly keeps Ed on his toes, but she will never run Demi Moore a close competition in the looks department. Nor did she turn flirty when Peabody fired off one of his compliments. On the contrary, she chose instead to ignore him and to attend to her griddle.

Each morning, Peabody would order the identical breakfast—juice, dry toast and a Western omelet, which he asked to have prepared without the yolks.

"We call that a white Western," Ed would tell him and Peabody would take note of that advisory, saying, "Yes, of course."

But the following day he would continue to ask for a Western omelet without the yolks.

"I'm not wrong in asking Betty to prepare them that way, am I?" he would say. "I'm not putting her to any trouble? Because I'd rather shoot myself in the foot than do that."

"Not at all," Ed would reply, although clearly it would have been much simpler for Betty to cook the eggs in a more conventional style. Indeed, from my vantage point, close to the grill, I could hear her mumbling under her breath: "Why can't he eat the fucking eggs like everybody else?"

After he had placed his order, Peabody would lean back, survey the diner and say: "I really love this place. I've tried the other diners in town, but this is the only one in which I feel comfortable. You don't *mind* my coming in here each day, do you?

"No, I don't," Ed would reply.

"Because if you do, I'll vanish, and you'll never see me again."

"There's no need for that."

And after all, what else could Ed say?

At no time did Peabody so much as look in my direction, which caused a certain amount of irritation on my part. No disrespect intended, but I felt confident that my life had been every bit as interesting and event-filled as Ed's. No, I do not own a diner. But I had the two-and-a-half years of wartime service to my credit. (Six months of it in 'Nam, among the Montagnards, with whom I still correspond.) There was also my trip to the newly formed Republic of Czechoslovakia, with a side excursion to the fleshpots of Hamburg (this was during the period in which I tried to find myself), not to mention the handshake I had once received from former secretary of agriculture, Ezra Taft Benson, during his inspection of our poultry facility.

The details of my early life are no less colorful. Having lost his tannery in a game of acey-deucey, my father, Andrew H. Binny, brought us over from Tennessee and quickly reestablished himself in an off-highway ramp convenience store that specialized in pickled sausages most agreed were of a gourmet quality. Along with his entrepreneurial skills, he had a bookish side, which he cultivated by installing a small lending library that stood apart from the pickling counter. When business was slow, he would don a stovepipe hat and a cape and read to me—

with wide rhetorical gestures—from his beloved Galsworthy, switching over now and then to the lovesick poems of Sir John Suckling, another favorite. In truth, it was the cape and the rhetorical gestures that I enjoyed the most. From time to time, I am told that my speech cadence is reminiscent of my father's—an observation that causes me to swell with pride.

My mother, Gertrude Binny, was a buxom somewhat ravaged-looking beauty who quickly adopted the flat nasal tones of America's heartland yet continued to miss the mountains of her beloved Tennessee. On occasion, she would disappear with one of the lending-library browsers, a circumstance my father bore up to with uncommon gallantry. I did not do as well and felt a cold wind on my neck until I saw her safely ensconced behind the pickling counter. (If it were up to me, I would have shut down the lending library and made people *buy* a few books for a change. And needless to say, I lost my appetite for pickled sausages.)

At happier times, accompanied by my father, my mother would leap atop a baby grand piano in the storage area and do a series of spirited Irish jigs.

All of this is but a mere sampling of my background and, of course, Peabody could know nothing of it—and continued to ignore me. It was almost as if he went out of his way *not* to notice me—which gave me the feeling that he was, indeed, aware of my presence. There is no question that he was of interest to me. There was his English accent, for one thing. I have always had a weakness for this manner of speaking, awarding extra points of intelligence to those who practice it. (Obviously this is absurd, since it is the content of an individual's speech that should be paramount.)

Then, too, there was the impression he gave off of casual affluence. Money—and how to get some—had been very much on my mind. When it came time to pay his check, he would reach into his pocket, pull out a bill and lay it on the counter without stopping to check its denomination. He generally paid with a ten or twenty, but on one occasion, a couple of hundreds fell out of his pocket and on to the floor. He did pick them up, but with impatience. His attitude seemed to be that financial matters, at least on a small scale, were of no interest to him.

ALL DOLLARS ASIDE (as if such a thing were possible), the more I thought about Peabody, the more I realized how badly I was in need of a new friend. Glo was gone, of course, and though my beloved daughter is interesting in a quirky way and came up with a new passion every day—such as cable-network anchor-woman—she obviously did not supply the kind of male companionship that I often require.

It was only recently that a freak accident had claimed the life of Irwin ("Little Irwin") Stubbs, my best and perhaps my only hanging-out type of friend. Little Irwin had just come off a successful gall-bladder operation and was leaving the hospital grounds when a beer truck appeared out of nowhere and to-taled his Subaru, killing Little Irwin instantly.

Talk about timing! Not only was his roofing business about to take off, but Little Irwin (a lifelong bachelor) had just started to keep company with a clothing buyer who was crazy about him, though she was twice his size. ("What I do is go up on her," he would say in his coarse yet somehow appealing style.) She would pat him on the head, pinch his fat little cheeks and generally make a big fuss over him, at least in public. They looked cute as hell together, but it was not to be. I attended the funeral ceremony, prepared to make some remarks about Little Irwin's vitality and overall zest for life—but the clothing buyer (who truthfully hadn't known Little Irwin that long) went on and on for what seemed like hours—and I was not called upon to speak. I held on to a copy of my remarks, but they were especially tailored to fit Little Irwin, and it is unlikely they will be suitable for another individual. (Maybe a few of them.)

I cannot tell you how much I missed the little hellraiser,

and as I soon learned, you cannot shake friends like Little Irwin down from a tree.

Was it any wonder that I was interested in making the acquaintance of Valentine Peabody—this intriguing newcomer to our community.

Chapter Two

I T WAS ED who set the wheels in motion for us to meet officially, although his gesture did not immediately have the intended effect.

One morning I arrived at the diner a bit earlier than was my usual custom and found that my place setting had been moved to the stool beside the one that was normally reserved for Peabody. Why this generous behavior on the part of Ed? Though he said nothing of it, I can only guess that Ed was aware that I had lost my job in poultry distribution, that my life was a lonely one—and that my daughter Lettie bristled when I showed the slightest interest in a female, even for the sake of companionship. No matter how hard I tried to disguise it, Ed, or so I felt, had seen the pain behind my eyes and responded accordingly.

Then, too, there is the nature of our town. Demographically we are at a crossroads, drawing some of our residents from the rambunctious western section of the state and others from our more sophisticated eastern corridor. There are hard-scrubbers among us from our barren northern tier along with easy-moving delta types from the alluvial south.

During the Civil War, we went this way and that way.

All of this might have resulted in a contentious brew—as it had in many of our great cities—but it has had the opposite effect on us.

Not long ago, we were voted "America's Third Friendliest City" by a spinoff of Forbes.

There is a man named Lowell Ginty in our town who has a head that is three times the normal size and a body that is not too appetizing to look at either. Let's just call him a human shipwreck. In some other community, he would probably be hidden away in an attic. Yet if you took the time to get to know him, you would find Lowell Ginty to be the most convivial of fellows and not in the least bit scary. In addition, he is something of an expert on the Harding administration.

Each day, Lowell Ginty takes his coffee and toasted English muffin at the Wal-Mart cafeteria where he is greeted warmly by early bird shoppers and left to his own devices.

Children who gawk at him are admonished.

I offer this as an example of our local style.

THE AMICABLE NATURE of our town notwithstanding, I could not resist asking Ed why he had arranged to seat me beside the quirky Valentine Peabody.

"I have always felt," Ed said cryptically, "that you should have a Continental friend."

With that, he joined Betty at the griddle, leaving me to puzzle over the meaning of his comment.

Peabody's reaction to the new seating arrangement was not what either of us expected.

He arrived a bit later, took a quick look at me and said: "This won't do. It won't do at all.

"What do you expect of me," he said, his face flushed and angry, "to just proceed and have my breakfast in this manner? Well, I won't, I can tell you that.

"And besides," he continued, running a hand through his luxuriant hair, "whose idea *was* it?"

"Certainly not mine," I said, gathering up my place setting and utensils and moving to the far end of the counter, hoping to indicate by my behavior that it would be fine with me if I never laid eyes on the man again. Though I could not think of any at the moment, I felt confident there were plenty of people who would enjoy my company.

"That's a bit more like it," said Peabody, taking his usual seat at the counter.

But his outburst seemed to have upset *him* as much as it did me.

"I didn't mean to hurt your feelings, Ed," he said, backing up a bit. "But it *was* a bit unusual, you have to admit that."

"You didn't hurt *my* feelings," said Ed, with a nod in my direction.

"Whatever," said Peabody, waving off Ed's response and somehow insulting me once again in the process.

"I mean here I'd been all prepared to have my breakfast in the usual manner," he said, "and then I come in and find *this*."

"Calm down," said Ed firmly. "What'll you have?"

"A white Western," said Peabody, in yet another concession.

I was feeling smaller and smaller, as if I'd been caught stealing from the cash register. And I was angry, too, so much so that it was all I could do not to bash Peabody. Which is what I probably would have done had I been a younger man. Ed took on an aloof attitude—since Peabody's outburst was as much a criticism of him as it was of me—and the atmosphere in the diner became chilly.

"I had an awful night," said Peabody, hunched over his food now—and giving more ground. "I generally have one martini before dinner and last night I must have had four.

"But I plan to work out this morning," he said, as if to reassure Ed of his excellent habits.

Ed's response was understandably muted and Peabody finished his omelet in a surprisingly sloppy manner, dabbing at the residue on his lips with a napkin.

"Now look here," he said to Ed, taking a bill from his pocket, examining it this time and then laying it on the counter. "I would like you to have a hundred dollars."

"Why is that?" asked Ed.

"I made a bet that Betty would come to work wearing the pink bedroom mules that I adore. Obviously she hasn't."

He gestured toward Ed's wife in the kitchen. She was wearing her standard flowered housecoat, but instead of the usual pink mules, she was trotting around in unlaced Nike sneakers and white sweatsocks.

"Ergo," said Peabody, "You win a hundred dollars."

Though I had never heard the word "ergo" pronounced aloud, I felt I had a good sense of its meaning. It had a nice ring to it, and I made a mental note to try to shoehorn it into one of my future conversations.

"But I didn't make any bet," said Ed, with some logic. "Therefore I cannot take the money."

"My dear fellow," said Peabody, trying to suppress his frustration. "I made a bet and *lost*."

"But I didn't *know* about the bet," said Ed, emphatically. "Therefore I did not win."

"Take the goddamned money," Betty cried out from the kitchen.

"Now there's a voice of reason," said Peabody with a triumphant smile.

"You stay out of this, Betty," Ed called out to his wife, a rare instance in which he had stood up to the peppery Nicaraguan.

In what must have been an act of desperation, Peabody glanced in my direction for support, but he might just as well have appealed to the sink. I certainly wasn't going to be of any help to him. Additionally, I sided with Ed; had I been in his position, I would have behaved in exactly the same manner. How can you accept money for winning a bet you never knew about and continue to think of yourself as an honorable man.

But Peabody evidently lived by some other code.

Seeing that his situation was hopeless, Peabody put the money back in his pocket and took a sip of coffee. Then his eyes went vacant. But he soon recovered and craned his head around, tilting up his chin as if he was listening to music. Then he turned to Ed, leaned across the counter in a conspiratorial manner and said: "Have I ever told you what a lovely place you have here?"

Chapter Three

AT ANOTHER TIME, I might have let the incident slide. But unemployment—and the promise it held of a bleak future—had dealt a sharp blow to my self-esteem. My way of dealing with the Peabody rebuke was to stay away from Ed's altogether and to take my breakfast at the cottage. It consisted of Special K cereal and 2 percent milk, for weight control—although I generally ended up eating several bowls of it and thereby invalidating the original purpose. More often than not, I would compound the felony by sneaking in a Linzer cookie. I would eat this breakfast on the porch and stare out at Liar's Pond where a distraught socialite had once met her end. Jamming on the brakes of her Jaguar XKE, she had leapt into the mire and gone to a watery grave. (It was never determined what was eating her.)

There were times when I wondered how much adversity it would take for me to join her down there.

"She certainly was brave," Lettie had said on the day Ed Bivens and his First Response Team went looking for her.

I immediately countered with the conventional litany about how it's much braver to soldier on through troubled times—since I did not want to give her any ideas for the future. But I knew what she meant.

Afternoons, I put in a few hours at the tanning salon where I had been placed in charge of registration and the timer. It is a much more responsible job than it would appear, my predecessor having been a hippie-type girl who got caught up in the music on her Walkman and fried a banker. (There had also been some talk that Megan was delivering more than suntans in the popular and oversubscribed cubicle four.)

The meager pay was not about to change my life, but there were excellent health-oriented magazines to be enjoyed in the reception area and other perks as well, such as reduced prices on sunblock creams. Free suntans were also available to the help, a privilege I rarely took advantage of, since I had no interest in walking around with some kind of slick Hollywood-style glow.

Later in the day, and with my heart in my throat, I would send off résumés to other poultry distributors. I had had them made up by an expert, and though each one was a typographical work of art, I did not feel that they captured the real me. To do that, you would have to spend some time in my company and gradually draw me out—which the résumé people were not inclined to do. But I had paid for the résumés, so I sent them out anyway.

After I had finished up at the salon, I would pick up Lettie at the middle school and bring her home. Upon arriving at the cottage, she would drink a glass of chocolate milk and then take up a position at the window, twisting her hands behind her and staring out at the pond.

"I have such an awful yearning," she would say with a sigh. "I want something, but I don't know what it is."

I recognized the dramatic tableau from a Disney made-for-TV movie, but I did not let on. Then, despite her not knowing what she wanted, she would present me with a wish list, a sample of which is as follows:

- New bedroom furniture
- The biggest trampoline they make
- A third cat
- A trip to Brentwood, California, Home of the Stars
- A Caboodle makeup kit

Apart from the Caboodle makeup kit, which I could manage, each item was like an arrow in my chest, since it was all I could do to hold on to the cottage. Lettie, who could detect the slightest dip in my spirits, would attempt to console me by saying, "They're just wishes"—but I took my responsibilities seriously, and had, ever since Lettie's mother had passed on.

THOUGH MY SITUATION at the moment was grim, I did what little I could to bolster my morale—dressing neatly, taking a daily shave and sponge bath, and even treating myself to such items as an ornate belt buckle. Sometimes I sent my clothing to the dry cleaners, despite the exorbitant cost. What exactly would I prove by giving up every last pleasure?

In this spirit, and taking advantage of one of Lettie's sleepovers, I drove out to Frolique one night. It is our only topless bar, and it is situated on a dark and deserted street in the farthest reaches of our town—as if everyone is ashamed of it. Though I still mourned the loss of Glo, I did not feel unfaithful by merely showing up there. Knowing her cheery nature, she might even have approved.

"You go right ahead, Binns," I could imagine her saying, "if that's what pleases you. But don't you dare sample the merchandise."

She would say this with a twinkle in her eye, one that she maintained throughout her darkest days. It's a wonder I have been able to push on without her—to the extent that I have.

We are a Bible Belt county, which explains why Frolique is the only establishment of its kind permitted in the region. And it was no walk in the park to get it through the legislature. Little Irwin had joined the Grimble brothers and several other party animals in standing outside the statehouse holding placards that said the bill better pass—or else!

It is probably easier to get into the Pentagon than it is to get past the door at Frolique. To be admitted, you must present a dozen different kinds of ID, be subjected to an interview and have your fingerprints put on file. That holds even if you have been there before. With all that hassle, you would think they had something special going on in there, which they don't.

Strictly speaking, it is not even all that topless, the two dancers who work there removing their halter tops only briefly at the conclusion of their act. One is a scrawny blonde with small titties and a sassy style. It is no strain to watch her. But on the night I showed up, Cassie was out of town on an industrial cleaning job. (It is not uncommon in our town for an individual to hold down two—or even three—jobs in order to make ends meet.)

The dancer on duty, Mary, is a hefty divorced mother of two who works as a receptionist during the day at the mortgage company. She has an excellent personality and never fails to greet customers with a bright smile—and to console them when their applications for a mortgage are turned down. But I have never been comfortable with her as a topless dancer. She has a broad-shouldered and squarish type of body that I have never found particularly appealing. (Which is not to suggest that she is a secret guy.) But maybe it is a failure on my part. Mary does have her fans—the Grimble brothers in particular—but none appeared to have shown up on this particular night. Whatever the case, she has a wonderful attitude and a good sense of rhythm.

And more important, watching her was something to do.

After filling out all the forms and establishing that I was not a felon, I ordered a beer at the bar and took a seat at one of the little tables in the lounge area. Then I settled in to watch Mary gamely shimmy and shake her big squarish body to a recording of ''Brown Sugar.''

I had the impression that I was the only member of the audience until the conclusion of Mary's dance, at which point I heard an individual at a table in the corner begin to stamp his feet, applaud loudly and shout, ''Bravo.''

The enthusiastic member of the audience turned out to be none other than my nemesis, Valentine Peabody.

To my surprise, he behaved in an unusually cordial manner toward me on this occasion. It was during Mary's break; no sooner had Peabody recognized me than he invited me over to his table and asked if I would join him in a glass of Mumm Champagne. I declined politely, saying I was aware that Champagne was a great treat, but I did not much care for it and preferred the Russian drink, Stolichnaya vodka.

He seemed taken aback at first, but after consideration, he asked if it was any good.

"It gets me by," I said.

"Really? Perhaps I'll try one as well."

He signaled to the fellow at the door who did the fingerprinting and also filled in as a waiter.

"Bring us two Stollies," said Peabody, pronouncing the name of the drink in an unusual way that frankly made me wince. Not that I would dream of correcting a fellow with an English accent.

When our drinks arrived, I automatically reached into my wallet to pay my share. Covering my hands with his own, Peabody leaned forward, stared deep into my eyes and said: "No, no, dear boy. *I'm* the host. You must remember that."

He proceeded to take a sip of his vodka, after which he licked his lips, and considered the taste.

"It's quite good, isn't it? I believe I'll be having some more of it in the future."

Then, his eyes shining with delight, he nodded toward Mary who had begun her second set.

"Isn't she marvelous. The manner in which she throws herself into her work with such abandon. I do believe she's quite extraordinary."

Suffice it to say that I did not agree with this evaluation of either Mary or her performance. "Serviceable" would have been much closer to it. But there is no accounting for taste, and I decided not to put a damper on my friend's enthusiasm.

"She gets the job done," was my diplomatic response.

"She does far more than that," said Peabody.

"I probably shouldn't say this," he continued leaning in

29

close to me, "but Mary quite fancies me. She's offered to come back to the hotel with me for $1,700. That's a bit high, don't you think?"

I certainly agreed with him and had no qualms about telling him as much. Then, too, I was surprised that Mary would make an offer of this nature, since I had always thought of her as a decent woman, her unhappy divorce and part-time career as a topless dancer notwithstanding. Still, I was not about to pass judgment on a struggling single parent. And there is no question that $1,700 would take you a long way in our community, particularly in these troubled economic times.

"It *is* awfully high," reflected Peabody, "particularly since I don't *need* her to come back to my hotel room. What I'd really like to do is be there when she gets out of the loo and smell her finger. Wouldn't *that* be something."

At this point, Peabody and I parted company in a serious way. He had entered a territory that was unfamiliar to me and one that I had no wish to explore. Not that it canceled out the possibility of our forging a friendship, but I could see that our tastes were light years apart. The last thing on earth I wanted to do was stand outside the loo and wait for Mary to come out so that I could smell her finger. Nor would I consider waiting outside the Paris Opera House for that purpose. Who would, for that matter, except this peculiar stranger who shared a table with me?

Yet once again, I saw no reason to throw cold water on the man's fantasies and muttered something noncommittal about different strokes being the order and strength of our nation.

"After all," I said, "isn't that what made America great?"

It was a comment that only served to provoke him.

"That's all very easy for *you* to say," said Peabody, with a wave of his hand. "With all your women."

Here again, I found him to be wide of the mark and had to wonder how he had formed the impression that I was a lothario. It was true that I had dated some as a bachelor and had the affair with a stuntwoman to my credit. But once I met Glo at the livestock auction, that was it for me in the romance department.

"I've done all right," I said with a modesty that was more than justified.

"I should say *so*," he said with a touch of self-pity.

"Now don't get me wrong," he said, recovering a bit. "I'm a great fuck."

"I never doubted it for a second," I said, wondering at the same time what it was that placed one in that enviable category.

"Those egg whites I have each morning help me along considerably," he said in partial answer to my unasked question.

"But I have to admit," he added with a chuckle, "my last lover fell asleep on me."

"It happens to the best of us," I said, though I had no evidence, either personal or otherwise, that it did.

Peabody then looked at me as if for the first time.

"You're a darling man, Binny," he said. "But you mustn't tell a soul that I've been here."

"It's not as if I'm going to leak it to 'Hard Copy,' " I said, instantly regretting the mild sarcasm.

"No, no, I'm quite serious. If word ever gets out, it will have a devastating effect on my life."

Before he could elaborate, Mary concluded her act by shaking her broad shoulders, whipping off her halter top, and treating the audience to a glimpse of her squared-off titties. Then she took a bow and shimmied off stage.

With barely a glance at her, Peabody looked at his watch.

"I'd better call for a cab," he said. "People don't realize it, but my work demands a great deal of energy."

I WONDERED, OF course, what kind of work it was that he did. Early on, I had formed the impression that he was involved somehow with the statehouse—but he did not seem to be the political type. Then I began to picture him as part of a computerized global enterprise with an office in our unfinished high-rise office building whose backers had been forced to halt construction when the S&L debacle hit. But it is not in my nature to ask probing questions. I assumed he would tell me what he did when and if he became ready.

Then, too, it struck me as odd that he would want to get around in a cab when it would have been an easy matter to take advantage of our highly affordable rent-a-car service. He was, of course, a fidgety kind of fellow, subject to sudden mood swings—and this was a style that would not have served him well behind the wheel. Since I had no particular interest in seeing Mary trot out for another go-round, I decided to offer him a lift back to the hotel.

"That's tremendously kind," said Peabody, as he carelessly tossed some money on the table. "But are you sure you don't want to get back to your lovely daughter?"

To the best of my knowledge, I had not mentioned Lettie to Peabody and wondered how he knew about her. A simple explanation was that Ed, who thought she was a beauty, and was always patting her on the head, had passed a remark about her at the diner.

"It's on the way," I said, and let it go at that.

We walked out to the parking lot, and he waited for me at the entrance while I brought the Trooper round. It was immaculate both inside and out, as bright and shiny as a new penny. As my situation worsened, I had considered trading it in for a cheaper model—but it was my one indulgence and of great importance to my self-esteem. One of my pleasures was to see Lettie rise up with pride when I pulled up in the Trooper to pick her up after school. After a quick glance at her girlfriends, to make sure they were watching, she would slide into the passenger seat, as if she were a movie star. She called it our showoff car.

Peabody got in without comment, and we drove along in silence through a bleak section of town where our black citizens had erected candlelit memorials to their drug-related dead. He was hunched over, his eyes brooding and haunted, shivering a bit from a drop in the temperature. One of those droplets had formed at the tip of his sharp nose.

"I've been living in Karachi," he said, blowing on his hands. "But you probably know that."

Actually, I didn't, although it was one of the cities I longed to visit. I do not have an official Wish List, like Lettie's, but—my quick trip to the Republic of Czechoslovakia notwithstanding—I felt a certain sadness about not having seen hardly enough exotic places. (I have done my best to block out 'Nam.) Whenever I brought up a place like Bangkok to Little Irwin, he would punch me on the arm, then throw back his head dreamily and say: "The puss, Binny . . . Oh my God, all that puss."

And I would say, "No Little Irwin, that isn't it at all. I just want to see Bangkok."

But now it seemed I would never get there anyway.

"I didn't realize you were from Karachi," I said. "How is it?"

"I didn't say I was *from* there," he said, with a sharp glance in my direction. "I'm merely living there for a bit."

"Sorry about that," I said, not sure what I was apologizing for.

To the best of my knowledge it was not a crime to be from Karachi.

"I have a large studio," he said, as he calmed down and once again brought the conversation around to his own personal circumstances. "It has a small loft which I use as a bedroom. When my secretary comes over, we conduct our business in the studio area. That's quite enough space, don't you think?"

"I imagine it would get you by," I said, seeing that I was not going to get much more out of him on the subject of Karachi.

"I've just gone through a horrible and messy divorce," he said. "A noted film producer snatched my wife away from me. It was all over the press, reporters camping out on the doorstep, the Karachi equivalent of Charles and Lady Di, I would suppose. You probably read all about it in your own press."

"I may have, although we don't get much coverage of Karachi around here."

"You don't?" he said, sounding a little disappointed. "How surprising. In any case, you can understand that it was a relief for me to get away."

"I can see that it would be," I said, making a mental note to ask him at some future point why he had chosen our town of all places to get away to, rather than—as an example—the fabled and much glitzier Côte d'Azur.

"Apparently," he continued, "they'd been carrying on their affair for six years, and I never had the slightest clue. But then it's always that way, isn't it."

I said I agreed, but only in the interest of being sociable. Though I had no direct experience with infidelity, it seemed to me that in the course of an extended marriage you'd get some signs if there was any hanky-panky. Whenever I even *thought* about another woman—not that I did that often—Glo would be on my case in an instant, albeit good-naturedly, asking me what on God's earth had gotten into me.

"Were there children?" I asked.

"Six," he answered quickly. "All of them girls. All of them fucking since they were twelve."

At that point, I found myself gripping the wheel to make sure I didn't drive off the road. I thought of Lettie, sleeping over at the precocious Edwina's and was sorry I hadn't double-checked to make sure they were closely supervised. There was a rumor that Edwina had started "dating," and I knew what that meant. As if that wasn't bad enough, I'd heard that Edwina's mother had a new boyfriend and that, according to Lettie, he had dirty fingernails.

I made a note to call over there the minute I got home.

"You'd better get used to the idea, old boy," he said, apparently enjoying my consternation.

"That'll be the day," I said and thought of the half-serious pact I had made with Lettie, one that specified that she was not to go out with anyone until she was thirty.

How would I handle it, I wondered, if the unthinkable came to pass?

Peabody was staying at the Garfield Hotel, which is situated on Main Street in the center of town. As we approached it, he said he had brought up his unhappy domestic situation in the interest of explaining why it mustn't be known that he had frequented *Frolique*.

"Bettina and I have been exchanging letters of late," he said, "and there's a chance—only the slightest, mind you—that she might take me back. Her lover turns out to be something of a rake—he's not quite divorced—and he has huge family expenses. But if Bettina found out I'd been to a topless bar, that would be the end of it. So you mustn't breathe a word to a soul."

This line of reasoning got me so exasperated that I could hardly speak. The very idea of Bettina taking *Peabody* back—when *she* was the one who had behaved adulterously was laughable if not preposterous. Shouldn't it be the other way around, with Peabody graciously agreeing to take *Bettina* back? Assuming he was foolhardy enough to do so.

But obviously they had a different way of looking at things in Karachi.

It occurred to me as well that if their reconciliation could be threatened by a single visit on Peabody's part to a topless bar—which was just barely topless—then their future together was shaky indeed.

I decided it was time for me to stop sugarcoating my feelings and to speak to him in a forthright manner.

"Why would you want to be with a woman who'd drop you over an innocent visit to a topless joint?"

At this, Peabody virtually exploded with rage.

"Because," he shouted, *"she's got the best bum in Karachi, that's why."*

I held the wheel with one hand, and we glared at each other, jaw to jaw, neither of us giving ground.

Then the air went out of him.

"Who knows," he sighed, as we pulled up to the hotel, "perhaps you're right. You know so much about women."

THE GARFIELD WAS a once grand establishment that had long ago gone to seed. Yet it had character, and I could see why Peabody had chosen it over the more popular Spinelli Arms, a steel and glass structure that to my mind was an antiseptic monstrosity—though it did overlook the river.

Despite its general mustiness, the Garfield was known to be efficiently run and had one-of-a-kind antique furnishings in its oversized rooms. I had been inside the lobby and recalled that it featured a life-sized bust of Samuel Clemens (aka Mark Twain) at the entranceway. On a wall behind the registration desk there hung a signed photograph of Rita Moreno, the versatile dancer/actress having occupied the VIP suite on the occasion of a Lillian Gish Tribute at the convention center, or so the hotel claimed.

The doorman was a crusty and shriveled up little fellow who had been there since day one. If you asked him how he was doing, he would take off his cap, scratch his ear and give you the same answer: "I've seen them come and I have seen them go."

Since I knew what he would say, I did not ask him how he was doing.

He opened the door for Peabody, who got out and seemed to notice the Trooper for the first time.

"What a lovely vehicle," he said. "I can see that *someone's* getting along nicely."

"Not really," I said. "I have financial problems."

"Too much money?"

"Uh uh. Not enough."

"Really," he said as we shook hands in the lobby. "If that's the case, stay in touch.

"I can make you rich."

Chapter
Four

I CAN ASSURE you that Peabody's last words to me that night did not fall on deaf ears. To the contrary, I repeated them to myself all the way back to the cottage. It was the second time in my life that someone had made such a proposal to me, and I had good reason to remember the first.

It had come from a fellow named Ted Feather who worked alongside me at the poultry distributor. It was Feather's idea to break away from the firm and start up his own operation in Canada. Would I care to join him?

"If you do," he said. "I will make you rich."

He was an eager and rail-thin little pup of a fellow who was always trailing behind me, yipping at my heels—and I did not take him seriously. For one thing, he had approached me at the height of my career, a heady time during which I was carving out new routes in areas where it was thought to be impossible. This had gotten me the respect not only of my supervisor but of my enthusiastic little team of co-workers (they were called the Capons) as well. A raise had been put through for me, and there was talk of another. I thought it would never end. As if that wasn't enough, Glo was earning plaudits for her success in rehabilitating disabled storks—and other wildlife that everyone else had given up on. It would not have been an exaggeration to describe us as a regional Power Couple.

So naturally, I declined Ted Feather's offer.

Today, Feather sits on top of a conglomerate with far-flung interests not only in poultry but in such disparate fields as semiconductors and bakery goods as well. He thumbs his nose at the Japanese, and there has been a hint that he is behind a motion picture that is scheduled to star Patrick Swayze (assuming his people can come to terms with Swayze's people).

Had I taken Ted Feather seriously, I might be sitting beside him up there in Winnipeg with the world at my feet and not having to scrounge out a few dollars working the timer at some tanning salon.

I was not about to make the same mistake again.

Still, it surprised me that I had been so forthcoming about my difficulties with Peabody, a man I hardly knew. I had virtually thrown my situation in his face, which was not like me. One explanation is that I had been looking for a chance to say that I had "financial difficulties," a phrase I had picked up on CNN's *Money Line,* hosted by Lou Dobbs. It put me in the company of hot new organizations that had grown too fast and were strapped for funds. And it sounded more dignified than saying you were tapped out—or had to get your hands on some money fast.

But more to the point, I had exhausted my meager savings and I was desperate.

Several years before, I had placed my small retirement fund in the hands of a gentleman named Abner Teitlebaum, whose silvery hair, soft voice and crinkly eyes made him out to be a pillar of conservatism. His gentle, soothing style on the phone only served to heighten that impression. But these characteristics proved only to be the facade of a reckless high roller. In short order, he had invested my money (and that of several other poultry workers) in a string of Filipino condos that not only failed to attract a target group of German tourists, but was soon swept away in a monsoon.

To his credit, Teitlebaum suffered a nervous breakdown and now resides in a private clinic in Costa Rica, presumably beyond the reach or interest of US authorities.

I have always had great respect for our Jewish brothers, unlike some in our community I prefer not to name. Yet I cannot help but place some responsibility for my present situation at the feet of Abner Teitlebaum. (Though I am unable to say with any certainty that he ever practiced Judaism actively or not.)

At that point in my life I had worked long and hard and played by the rules only to wind up with little or nothing. I had not lost faith in my country and prayed I never would. Try naming a better one. India? Norway? I rest my case. Yet there I was, having given over the best of my years to poultry distribution, with no future whatsoever.

Apart from the knee, I was in good health and considered myself to be an excellent piece of manpower. Certainly there should have been a place for me, but it appeared there wasn't. Had the country let me down? I would never say such a thing, although others might.

Whatever the case, I was determined not to let opportunity slip through my fingers a second time. The first chance I got, I planned to remind my new friend of his offer—and to find out if there was any substance to it—or if he was blowing smoke.

SINCE THERE WAS no longer any reason to stay away from Ed's, I showed up at the diner the next morning and found Peabody there—in a state of high agitation. He stood beside his usual stool, tapped his foot and drummed his fingers on the counter as if he could not make up his mind if he should stay or go. Clearly relieved that I had shown up, he threw his arms around me and gave me a light kiss on the cheek, which I could easily have done without.

"I'm so glad you've come," he said as we both sat down on our stools. "I'm just not comfortable when you're not about."

This represented a dramatic change in his attitude toward me, but I was getting used to his lightning changes of mood and chose not to remind him that he had been outraged when I first sat down beside him.

"I'm not being treated well," he said. "Ed has totally ignored me. It's just not the same, Binny, trust me on that."

I looked around and saw that the diner was more crowded

than usual, a considerable number of fellows from out of state having shown up for the feed show.

"It's probably because he's got his hands full."

To prove my point, I signaled over to Ed, who lumbered forward to take our order in the usual manner. As Ed stood over us with his pad, Peabody looked up at him shyly, as if he was hoping for a sign of affection.

When our orders arrived, Peabody picked at his white Western omelet for a bit and then shoved it aside.

"This won't do," he said. "Ed is obviously annoyed at me and I haven't the foggiest notion why. I can't go on this way, Binny."

I looked over at Ed again and saw that he did seem a little detached. He was always detached, but it was possible he was more detached than usual. But what difference did it make if he was detached or not? Or if he was annoyed at Peabody? With all due respect, it was not as if Ed Bivens was the mayor. I suggested as much to Peabody, who raised his voice and said, "It makes a great deal of difference. We've known each other for years. And I simply can't continue on in this way, with Ed behaving so horribly."

It came as news to me that he and Ed had a past relationship, but it did explain, though only in part, what Peabody was doing in our community.

"Maybe I'll just go over there and bash his face in," said Peabody.

Though I did not believe for a second that he was capable of such behavior, I put my hand on his arm in gentle restraint.

"There's no need for that."

I gave some thought to the situation, and it occurred to me that Peabody and I, sitting together as we were, appeared to be old friends and confidants. Was it possible that Ed felt left out of the party? Even though he was the one who had brought us together? Men are often like that. He may have heard that we'd spent the night at Frolique and been offended that we had not asked him along—not that Betty, who kept Ed on a tight rein, would countenance such an excursion.

Acting on a hunch, I asked Ed if he would care to sit with us.

"Why, thanks," he said, and even though the place was hopping, he took a seat beside us.

"So, *that's* what it was." Peabody cried out in an agonized wail, causing some of the out-of-state fellows to wheel around in our direction.

"For God's sake, Ed," he continued, his voice cracking with emotion. "Why didn't you *say* you wanted to join us? How were we to know? If we'd had so much as a hint of your distress, we would have been only too happy to include you in our plans. Binny *adores* your company. You *know* how *I* feel about you. You have such a lovely place here, have I told you that?

"Betty," he called out to the kitchen. "You've a very pretty face, really you do. There's no need for you to get down on yourself about your appearance."

Betty looked at him as if he was insane. Muttering something along the lines of "stupid asshole," she started scraping the griddle in a violent manner. Ed and I squirmed with embarrassment and half the place stared at us.

Ed put his head in his hands and said, "I can't deal with the fucker. I never could."

Then he got up from his stool, shifted the position of his big belly, and walked behind the counter.

"Oh, dear," said Peabody. "I've done something wrong again, haven't I? Perhaps I should have another go at him."

"Eat your eggs," I said, and dug into my own.

When we had finished our breakfast and the crowd had begun to thin out, I took a sip of coffee and brought the conversation around to his proposal of the night before.

"What exactly did I say?" he asked, still looking nervously over at Ed.

"That you could make me rich," I said, marveling at my directness.

"Oh, yes," he said vaguely. "I suppose I did say something along those lines.

"Well, come along then," he said, getting up from his stool. We can't very well discuss it here, not given Ed's horrible attitude toward me."

HE CALMED DOWN somewhat after we had left the diner, but I remained on guard all the same since I had never met such a sensitive individual in my life. And you never knew when you would get another one of his eruptions.

To work off our breakfast, we took a walk along the river, which trailed through the center of town in a picturesque manner while serving no particular purpose. Though we had once been a dynamic hub for interstate commerce, all such traffic had dried up long ago, with the coming of the air age. Peabody led the way, and we cut through the Indian Memorial Park, a tourist attraction that rarely attracted anybody; the attendant in charge practically had to grab people off the street to get them to look at the tomahawk display. Then we walked along the shabby stores of Main Street, many of them boarded up casualties of the new mall. There was a tuxedo store that had managed to survive and another that repaired caneback chairs—but that was about the size of it. The deterioration of Main Street is not just *our* story, it is an *American* story, and one that had better be reversed if we are to survive as a nation. And don't tell me about cyberspace. That alone is not going to do it.

"You seem to know the area pretty well," I said.

"I bloody well should. My grandfather owned a place in the hills, and I spent many a happy summer there as a boy. Ed doesn't recall this—or prefers not to—but he and I skinny-dipped together on several occasions and laid out on the rocks afterward, dreaming of the future, discussing our cocks and the like. I'm sure you've often done that sort of thing with a friend.''

Actually, I hadn't. And I could not even *imagine* lying out on the rocks and discussing cocks with Little Irwin, for example, who, as it happened, was hung like a horse. We had discussed pussy, of course, as is only normal. As a matter of fact, that's *all* Little Irwin wanted to discuss—but we drew the line there. Still, I let Peabody go on.

"Ed was quite something to look at then, a bit of an Adonis, really, not that there was anything between us of a sexual nature. I looked him up when I came back to settle my grandfather's estate and was delighted to see he'd chosen Betty as his wife. She's quite formidable, don't you feel?''

I nooded in agreement since she was certainly that. And Betty was fine if you needed someone to crack a whip and keep you in line. Or if you favored stocky little Nicaraguan pepper pots in general. But bless her—and may she live to be a hundred and have the immigration laws turned in her favor—she had never been my particular cup of tea. And I was not alone. I had heard others say: "Hey, Ed, *you're* the one who has got to live with her, am I right?'' To which Ed would stick out his jaw truculently and say: "You're fuckin' A.''

I did not know Ed during his formative years, having been brought over from Tennessee when I was ten—so it was difficult for me to envision the porked-up, and quite frankly, slovenly proprietor of our diner, as some kind of Greek god. And I did not particularly want to think about the youthful pair lying around bareassed discussing their dicks . . . But at least I had a more detailed explanation now as to why Peabody had shown up in our community rather than the many trendier locales that were obviously available to a man of his means.

PEABODY'S OFFICE WAS on the top working floor of our high-rise office building, the last one to be constructed before the devel-

opers ran out of funds. It was much as I had pictured it—a large
airy space, sparsely but expensively furnished with a long steel
desk, a state-of-the-art computer, a bank of phones, a stereo console and a screen and slide projector. What was unusual was that
the walls were decorated with black-and-white photographs that
appeared to have been taken at the time of the Weimar Republic in Germany, a period in history that had always fascinated
me.

Among the subjects depicted were a midget on a towering
unicycle, a grinning impresario with clown makeup and a gold-
toothed dancer in black lingerie and spiked heels, standing with
her legs apart and taunting a man who lay on the ground in
handcuffs, looking helplessly up at her crotch.

Unless I was mistaken, the fellow being humiliated bore an
uncanny resemblance to Valentine Peabody.

This jarring touch notwithstanding, I admired the harsh
beauty of the photographs and thought about asking Peabody
for a duplicate set of prints. Obviously they would conflict with
the essentially French Provincial-style that Glo had designed for
the cottage, but I felt confident that I would be able to work
them in.

The overall decor at the office confirmed my feeling that
Peabody was involved in something global, with a possible S&M
twist to it.

Peabody offered me one of the two leather chairs and got
right down to business.

"I work for a chap name Gnu. Thomas Gnu. He's an enormously wealthy man—arguably the richest in the world, although he prefers to keep a low profile—you won't find him
showing up in Forbes, for example. I suppose I shouldn't, but
I'll let you have a quick look at him.

"Not a word about this," he said, as he removed a slide
from his desk.

"You can count on it," I said, with some irritation, since he

seemed to think I was going to reach for the phone every time
he scratched his nose!

Peabody inserted the slide in the projector and then put
on some Charleston-style music, which I felt was unnecessary,
since it did not go with the image on the screen. But for reasons
of his own, he seemed to be trying to create some kind of jazzy
Weimar-style mood.

The man on the screen was a shriveled-up fellow who wore
a black turtleneck and a black suit jacket that was several sizes
too big for him. So much so that his little fingers barely pro-
truded from the jacket sleeves. His skin was chalk white, and he
had a full head of black hair, *too* full actually, which led me to
believe he was wearing a toupee. His face had a simian quality to
it, and he did not look happy, which I could fully understand,
judging from his appearance.

All in all, he came across as one of those ancient commis-
sars who always sat glumly in the background while someone
like Brezhnev made a speech.

What ever happened to those fellows, I wondered, now that
the Soviet Union has fallen apart?

"He's quite something, isn't he?" said Peabody.

"He's no Cary Grant."

"He's not *feeling* very well these days," said Peabody, somewhat in defense of his employer.

Then he turned down the music and switched off the projector.

"He'd been ill for some time and given up for dead. Several of his associates were all for pulling the plug when I
stepped in and argued successfully against it. When Gnu recovered and heard what I'd done, he fired the whole bloody lot of
them and appointed me his chief aid and confidant."

Though Peabody's story had a dark side to it, I realized, as
I listened to it, that I was thoroughly enjoying myself. It was the
first time I had ever been close to money and power on a global

scale—though, of course, no business had as yet been trans-acted.

"He's quite a bitter man," Peabody continued, "as you can well imagine. Gnu has no family to speak of, and his sole re-maining goal in life is to settle the score with several of his old adversaries, enemies, really—which is why I thought you might be able to help us."

At this point, I could feel myself getting agitated, but I tried to remain casual, as if I was no stranger to conversations of this kind.

"In what capacity?" I asked.

"At first, Gnu handed me a list that was a yard long—he's accustomed to working on a large canvas. But I told him it wasn't practical and had him winnow the group down to a hand-ful of the more disagreeable candidates. We decided to start with a chap named Dickie Moué who tormented him at Groton, mercilessly teasing him about his multiracial origins and circu-lating photographs of Gnu's tiny penis.

"One night, just as Gnu was about to lose his virginity to a townie, Moué barged into their motel room with a choral group and led them in a chorus of "Everything Happens to Me."

As it happened, I remembered the first verse of the popu-lar Forties ballad, a classic in self-pity.

> *I make a date for golf*
> *and you can bet your life it rains*
> *I try to throw a party*
> *and the man upstairs complains*
> *I guess I'll go through life*
> *just catching colds and missing trains*
> *Everything happens to me.*

"The poor bastard," I said, and quickly realized the irony of my showing sympathy for a fellow who had more money than God.

"It was quite awful," Peabody agreed. "As a result of the motel episode, Gnu became impotent for decades and oddly enough, it's only in recent years that he's regained some measure of virility. Likes blowjobs and the like, although frankly I don't see why, having never cared for them myself."

Peabody's admission puzzled me. I thought back to my experience with Glo who would volunteer now and then to oblige me in that area (and then roll her eyes in exasperation as if *I* was the one who had brought it up—and that I was some kind of naughty fellow for doing so). My point is—the very *idea* of a desirable and highly intelligent woman (who should have known better?) licking away at my privates had to be one of the high points of my life, far exceeding any successes I had achieved in poultry distribution. How awful could I be if some bright-eyed charmer was willing to do that for me!

Apart from special occasions such as anniversaries and birthdays (mine, of course), Glo kept them short and sweet (early on we called them "hors d'oeuvres, then we took to labeling them "starters") and who could blame her. She also never failed to remind me of my good fortune, pointing out that most women do not really like to deliver them up—and only do so as an accommodation.

"Believe me," she would say. "I have checked with my girlfriends."

That came as a surprise to me, and was disappointing in that it cast doubt on the motives behind the occasional treat I had lucked into during my bachelor days. But I took her word for it and recalled, in support of her position, the night Myron Grimble, one of the Grimble brothers, had stood up at Frolique, his body shaking with anguish, and announced: "I have never gotten a blowjob."

Little Irwin was so moved by this pitiful admission that he offered to rush right out and see if he could set one up that very night. Myron's brother, Vernon, was not half as charitable.

"Sit down, you fool," he said, yanking at his brother's sleeve. "You do not make such announcements in public."

That, of course, was easy for Vernon to say since it was widely known that he was a rubber-bones and could give *himself* blowjobs.

But maybe I had led a privileged life after all.

PEABODY CONTINUED TELLING me about Thomas Gnu's early humiliations.

"Now none of this may seem like much to you, but Gnu has been smarting over these incidents for years."

"I can see why. And I can understand why he'd want to get back at the fellow. If it were me . . ."

"He wants Dickie Moué eliminated," said Peabody cutting in sharply, "and I thought you might be just the fellow to see it through. We'll pay you a fee of $175,000 with an advance of $75,000, and the balance upon completion. If you like, we can have the funds transferred to your account in CDs."

I was amazed. Was it possible I was the one he was talking to? Or was it a case of mistaken identity? Yet there it was—*whoever* he was talking to—right out on the table. Unless I'd heard him incorrectly, Peabody was asking me, William H. Binny, who had never so much as run a stop sign, to take the life of a fellow human being, though in truth, the swinish Dickie Moué might not answer to that description.

I could feel myself starting to get dizzy and I hoped I was not about to faint, which I have done before in moments of great stress. My father had been a fainter as well—particularly during his Tennessee days—and had trained my mother to revive him by pulling at his nose when he lost consciousness.

I let a few seconds go by while I collected myself, making it seem I was sorting out a variety of proposals that had been offered to me and trying to decide which one to pick.

"I don't know about the CDs," I said finally, as if that was the one consideration that had been holding up my decision.

"Whatever," he said with a dismissive wave.

I felt a follow-up question was called for at this point and decided to ask the most logical one.

"Why me and not a professional?"

"We considered that option, of course, and rejected it. These people have a way of coming back to you. You're never quite rid of them. There are demands for more money—and that's the least of it. You become entangled with their associates. It all becomes very messy. We wanted someone out of the stream."

"I'm certainly that, all right."

"And besides, you're quite professional. I've always admired your work—you're quite brilliant at it—take on a task, finish it through. Now that I've had the pleasure of meeting you, I couldn't be more convinced that you're the man we've been looking for."

It was clear that my background had been investigated. And it was no accident that Peabody and I had come together at the diner. No doubt he had contacted Ed and asked him to come up with someone in the community who was a little desperate and short of funds—and Ed had selected me. Then Peabody—with Ed's help—had arranged for us to hook up, as if by chance. Peabody had been playing me like a fish, and I had innocently gone for the bait.

As for his knowledge of my so-called brilliance on the job— that could only mean that he had gotten his hands on my efficiency report at the poultry distributor—one that had given me the equivalent of rave reviews. (When I first saw it, I could hardly stand to live with myself.) It was intended to be a private communication, but considering Peabody's global capabilities, it would have been child's play for him to tap into it.

"You didn't happen to see my ER, by any chance?"

"I don't read," he said quickly, as if it were a point of

pride. "A bit of Shakespeare now and then, some Neruda, but that's the lot. My sister may have gotten a look at it. *She's* the reader."

He paused, then said: "You don't happen to have read any good books lately, have you."

"The Plague," I answered quickly, and without thinking, as if one had been visited upon me. Considering the nature of his proposal, it was probably no accident that I had chosen the most desolate work that the Frenchman Camus had ever come up with.

"Sounds fascinating," said Peabody. "I'll ask my bookseller to reserve a copy."

At this point, I felt I'd had enough and decided to put an end to the discussion before I got in any deeper.

"I'm enormously flattered," I said, realizing I sounded a little like Peabody, "but there's no way I can see my way clear to do this."

"I rather thought that would be your initial response," he said, "but do take some time to consider it. You haven't been heard from, so to speak, for quite a while, and you don't want to be shortsighted and disappear from the screen entirely. Think of it as an investment in your future."

I could see now that Peabody was aware of my desperate job search—which had come to nothing despite the high quality (and expense) of my résumé.

"I do have some work," I said, trying to summon up some pride.

"Oh, yes, I'd quite forgotten your responsibilities at the *suntan* emporium."

He said this with a raised eyebrow and that slight hint of contempt that the English are able to convey so effectively. Since that's about all they've got these days, you can see why they cling to it.

"How much time do I have?" I asked, aware that I had left the door open a crack.

"We'd like to move on this as soon as possible. Dickie's in Miami now, and it would be useful to catch him before he leaves for St. Bart's. Suppose you sleep on it and call me tomorrow.

"I'd very much like to work with you," he said, coming over to give me one of his hugs. "In addition to all your other qualities, you have such a lovely smell."

I cannot explain why I was embarrassed by the sudden compliment. Yet embarrassment was what I felt, and the best response I could manage was a self-conscious "Why thank you, sir."

Chapter
Five

S TILL, I COULD not help being flattered that Peabody had admired my cologne. After my banner year at the distributor, the Capons had sent away to Dunhill in Manhattan for a bottle of their finest after-shave lotion, which was presented to me at a fish fry in my honor. (I was roasted at the affair, and by the time they finished working me over with such good-natured taunts as "Binny is in a class by himself—and we hope he stays there"—I was one cooked piece of poultry.

The cologne had been a big hit at Frolique, Mary picking up on it from her position on stage, some thirty feet away from me. She suggested that Myron Grimble consider dousing himself with a bottle if he was serious about wanting to meet her after work. (I took all of this as a hint to apply it in a more subtle way in the future.)

But I was coming to the end of my supply and had started to worry about the cost of a refill. As foolish as it may sound, I did not want to take a step back on colognes.

As I left Peabody's building, I found myself looking around on all sides to see if the police were on my trail. There was an old trick I remembered from somewhere about turning your windbreaker inside out when you were being followed—to throw the pursuer off your trail. I almost put it into play, but I decided that this was going too far—since all I had done so far was listen. Imagine how I would behave if I had actually committed a crime! But no doubt this was part of my appeal to Peabody—the fact that I had a clean slate and would be the last person in the world anyone would suspect of being a cold-blooded killer. The same holds true of my appearance, the way that I can just blend into a crowd. You had to know me for a while before my pale face and bland features came into focus. My own mother had once mistaken me for one of her secret dates. If my brown eyes had not appealed to Glo, I might never have been able to snap her up.

For the time being, I decided to take no action and to follow the spirit of one of the slogans I had pasted up on the refrigerator: ENJOY THE MOMENT. I had twenty-four hours to make up my mind, and there was no point in jumping into something that could have disastrous consequences.

I PICKED UP Lettie later in the day and took her back to the cottage, where I found seven real-estate agents waiting on the porch. I had put the house up for sale, mostly to see how I would do if I had to sell it in an emergency, which I felt I was in. I had not bargained on quite so many agents showing up and was puzzled by their interest. It was just a two-bedroom shack with a dock attached to it, even though Liar's Pond was a hundred yards away and wasn't deep enough for a boat anyway. With her artful arrangement of throw pillows and wild flowers, Glo had turned that little shack into a jewel box. No one believes me on this, but I have always felt that with the proper backing Glo could have given Martha Stewart a run for her money. But there is no need to speculate about that now. Neither Lettie nor I possess her knack—and the house looks it.

The agents had obviously been trained to play their cards close to the vest. They fanned out across the house, took a quick look around and then fanned back out with grim expressions on their faces. If they had found oil on the property, they certainly weren't letting on. The head agent lingered a bit and said that the nearby Liar's Pond was a selling point, in no small part because of the famous socialite who had chosen it as the body of water in which she wanted to take her life.

"If anyone is interested," she said, "I'll try to keep their attention focused on the pond and away from the house."

After they were all gone, I popped a frozen macaroni and cheese dinner into the microwave for Lettie. It was her favorite, and I kept a supply of them on hand, while at the same time lecturing her on the importance of green vegetables. But she was still a lanky thing, so I didn't worry too much about it.

When she had finished her dinner, she went into her room to do her homework, and at the same time to sing along with a recording of the Broadway musical classic, *Guys and Dolls*. Doing both at the same time was a trick that she was able to pull off. Based on what I heard, I did not foresee much of a career for her on the Broadway stage, but I had to admire her courage.

I made myself a bologna sandwich on rye, making sure to slap on a thick layer of mustard; new findings had established that it was healthier for you than mayonnaise, and I wanted to take advantage of that.

Then I settled in for the seven o'clock news, wondering as I watched it, why the networks felt it had to be delivered by a fellow with a facelift and a toupee. Their thinking seemed to be that it had more authority to it when it was served up by a fellow who was attempting to look like a young pup. And that no one wanted to hear from an individual who had accumulated years of wisdom and experience. That, of course, made no sense to me. Still, I felt dutybound to watch it each night for fear I would miss something—although how it helped my situation to know about who was starving where—and to be brought up to speed on ethnic strife in Burundi—is something I cannot say for sure.

"How are things?" Lettie asked as I sat beside her on the bed.

It was an innocent enough question, and no doubt one that is asked regularly in households all over America. But Lettie had never asked it of me before, which led me to believe that she sensed something was up.

"I've got to make an important decision," I said.

"Maybe I can help you," she said. "What I do is write down all the pluses on one side and the bad stuff on the other. Then I see which side is longer and make up my mind."

It wasn't a bad idea, and I said I'd try it. Then I tucked

Lettie in and gave her forty or fifty kisses, followed by a series of send-off hugs. We may have our flaws, but there is no family unit I know of that exchanges more hugs. She fell asleep immediately, and I stared at her, happy that she was the image of Glo and at the same time wondering where I fit into the picture. (Not that it ever crossed my mind for a second that she didn't belong to me. Glo wasn't like that. And when, in her busy schedule, would she have found the time?)

I'd begun to see a slight resemblance around the cheek-bones, so maybe that was it.

With Lettie safely off to bed, I went out on the dock, looked over at Liar's Pond and confronted my dilemma.

It was uncanny—but Peabody had hit just the right figure—$175,000. The most I had ever earned in any given year was $28,500, and I was now being offered approximately six times that figure. My dreams had never been to enrich myself, only to get along and to achieve inner peace. Thus far, I had been unable to pull off those modest goals. If Lettie and I kept our costs down, then $175,000 is all the money we would ever need.

And it wasn't as if I doubted my ability to do a job of any kind once I set my mind to it. Witness my organization, year after year, of our award-winning poultry exhibition. So Peabody had done his research in that department.

As for Dickie Moué, I'd heard enough to know that he was the kind of fellow that I did not much care for. He had probably ended up in the world of finance, had never done an honest day's work and probably increased his earnings by around $50,000 before he rolled his fat ass out of bed in the morning— with never a thought to those of us who weren't born with a silver spoon. It's possible he had changed his stripes, but that type rarely does.

Was there any doubt that the world would be a better place with one less of his kind?

I skipped over the precise means I would employ in getting rid of him, thinking I would deal with that when the time came. There was a chance I would get caught, of course, which is why they were offering me all that money. But considering my unblemished record, and my honorable service in the military, it was unlikely I would get the chair. Being incarcerated would give me a chance to read to my heart's content, catching up with classics such as *The Mill on the Floss,* and Trollope's forty novels—of which I had only waded through a couple.

I might even write a screenplay about the experience, all profits going to Lettie.

But could I take the life of another individual, even someone as obnoxious as Dickie Moué? The answer was yes, providing my life or that of a loved one was in jeopardy. But since neither was the case, it would be tough sledding.

I went to bed and tried to lose myself in Emerson's *Essays,* which I thought would be homespun, but turned out to be a tough read. It did prove to me that our American writers could be every bit as complex as their European counterparts. But I fell asleep anyway, only to wake up two hours later, and to find myself back on square one.

Lying there in the darkness, I longed for Glo to be there at my side so she could advise me, although had she been, she probably would have said: "Can't it wait till morning? I'm so exhausted."

But if I had kept after her and told her it was *really* important, I knew what she would have said:

"If you really want to do it, Binns, you go right ahead. Just be careful."

She had never scolded me, her only concern being my happiness. It would not have mattered if I had proposed crossing the Atlantic in a bathtub. If that's what I wanted, I could count on her support.

But of course she was dead.

* * *

WHEN I FIRST met Glo I was dating a stuntwoman named Cindy who was considerably younger than I was and a constant source of delight. We met on the occasion of our company catering lunches for the crew of a made-for-cable prairie mini-series that was being filmed in our community. Cindy was a local girl who had been hired to do leaps from a silo for the director, who wanted to get the scene just right and kept asking her if she would try it one more time. So naturally she had worked up a big appetite by the time she arrived at our catering table. I saw to it that her plate was piled up high (with Chicken à la King), and we struck up a conversation—which led to our becoming friends—and then lovers.

Whenever we went out on a date, it was great fun to watch her suddenly leap over a parked car or crash through a double thermopane window and come out the other side, casually brushing little shards of glass off her bomber jacket. Cindy was tall and rangy and tremendously agile and inventive in bed, although she was reluctant to do formal stunts during our intimate moments. For example, if I asked her to grab on to some overhead appurtenance and vault out at me, she would decline, saying, "That's what I do at work."

If I had to look for a more serious flaw in her bedroom style, it would be that she tended to announce what I was doing while I was doing it. For example, she would say: "You are now removing my panties" or "You have just licked my ass," which of course I knew I had just done. It was as if she were broadcasting events at a stock car rally. But apart from that, we were great friends and although we did not see each other exclusively—she was also dating a chef—I sensed that she felt we would end up being Much More Than That.

Finally, however, the age difference became a factor in our romance. I could tell Cindy all about Lyndon Johnson's legislative prowess, for example, but there was very little she could tell me, other than about her girlfriends and their plans for the summer.

We were generally together on Sunday nights when she was not called upon to do stunt work. But on one such evening, I told Cindy I felt like being alone for a change, which I did. So I proceeded to be alone for a while, but when that did not satisfy me, I found myself inexplicably wandering out to the hog auction. And it was there that I met Glo. Was it love at first sight? All I know is that when she got up from a feed sack and fixed her clear, though watery, green eyes on me, I said to myself: "This is it."

I had said those words to myself before, but on those occasions I had been a little wrong. Not this time.

You could make the argument that Glo was not as pretty as Cindy—and believe me, my wife was no dog—but that was beside the point. I had never felt more comfortable with a member of the opposite sex. And I don't know what possessed me to think it was possible, but I thought she and Cindy could be friends and we could all hang out together. I actually took both Cindy and Glo to Little Irwin's Christmas party, and believe me, Little Irwin almost shit in his little pants when he saw us all walk in together.

"You're banging *both* of them?" he whispered to me, his beady eyes popping out of his head. "Binns, you are a horny bastard, and I am proud to be your friend."

Things went well for a while, with Glo and Cindy chatting each other up as if they were sorority sisters. But then, halfway along in the party, Cindy called me over to the punch bowl and said: "She's not half good enough for you, Binns."

I thought she was wrong, of course, that Glo was around twenty times *too* good for me, and I slowly began to see more of Glo and less of Cindy. One day Cindy called and said she had quite the mini-series and was moving on to Wyoming. I wished her well, and she said: "And by the way, you are a lousy fuck."

I wrote off the remark as being a product of hurt feelings

. . . or at least I hoped it was. In any case, that was the last time I spoke to Cindy, although I hear that she is now the president of a regional stuntwoman's association, acting in an administrative capacity and no longer called upon to do stunts.

Glo and I moved in together, and for the first time I found I could relax around a woman. There was no need to worry about a little extra hip fat or to twirl up my hair in a seductive manner. If I skipped an occasional full body sponge bath, it was not as if war had been declared. Glo would dole out just as much affection as if I had scrubbed myself from head to toe. And never once did I catch her wrinkling up her nose with displeasure. Nor did Glo herself feel the need to resort to cosmetic beauty. She had enough confidence in herself—and our love—to be a little on the unkempt side, trusting me to see through her raggedy appearance to the individual inside whom I loved. And when she decided to step on the gas and wear something decent for a change, she could hold her own with the best of them.

We got along so well that once in a while, just for variety, I would try to start up an argument by saying something along the lines of, "I can't take it any longer," and she would refuse to take the bait. In frustration, I would wind up loving her even more.

Glo continued her work in pet rehabilitation while I forged ahead in poultry. And then we got Lettie out of the deal, which put us over the top. I was grinning from ear to ear when they handed her to me, and I haven't stopped.

I should have known there is a limit to how much happiness we are allotted in this lifetime—and there is. One day, out of nowhere, Glo, who was as strong as a horse, began to cough and wither away. Sparing no expense, we had every kind of test done that they could come up with, and when the results came in, the doctor summoned us to his office and drew a picture of Glo's insides, with a little circle where he felt the trouble was.

When I saw that circle, I pitched over into a faint and had to be revived by both the doctor and Glo.

Anyone watching would have thought that I was the one with the circle.

Nothing much worked, including New Wave treatments just in from the Coast. Our last hope was a clinic in a distant community where they felt they had a shot at restoring Glo to her old self. I can recall vividly the day Lettie and I said goodbye to her. Arms around each other, we watched her go off with the nurses, bravely clutching her carryall and a copy of the new Vanity Fair. I started to cry and Lettie joined in, who knows, perhaps to show solidarity. Then we went off to a seafood restaurant and ordered two fried clam dinners.

"Are you sure it's all right to eat fried claims," Lettie asked, "when you've just checked a sick mother into a clinic?"

"Not only is it all right," I assured her, pushing the argument a bit, "but your mother would *want* us to eat fried clams."

One week later, a doctor with a foreign accent called and said they had identified the trouble as being the obscure malady called Mary's Lung. And in the same breath, he said she didn't make it and could we please make arrangements to come get her.

You can imagine how I felt. It was as if the ground beneath my feet had been snatched away. Yet there was Lettie to look after, and I could not, in good conscience, see my way clear to fall apart and have a complete nervous breakdown. So I sucked it up and pressed on. I told Lettie that in my view nobody really dies. We take on the characteristics of the ones we love and add them on to ourselves. In that sense, we are all given a chance at eternal life. Offhand, I could not think of any characteristics of Little Irwin's, for example, that I had added on to myself, although I'm sure there were some. But I did carry the best of Glo around with me and had conversations with her in my head that were as lively as if she were there.

None of this made much of an impression on Lettie who

obviously would have preferred to have the real Glo on hand rather than have to carry around her characteristics. She did not display much outward emotion in the days that followed—but every now and then, she would place a picture album on my lap—and then slip away without comment. It featured pictures of Glo growing up—as a skinny child, eyes full of wonder, as a sassy high-school cheerleader, kicking up her legs and innocently displaying her panties—at the dawn of her political consciousness during the sixties—when she had volunteered to be held overhead by her fellow student protestors and used as a human battering ram.

Despite my sorry situation, I do not have too many regrets in life. The one that I *do* have is that I did not know Glo during her formative years—and not just because she was a willowy thing who had not yet porked up. I envy those who did know her back then, boyfriends included, since I am not jealous in that particular regard.

Yet who knows, if we had crossed paths when she was a teenager, she might have passed me by without a glance. Fate had obviously arranged for us to meet when she was a little on the hefty side.

Nonetheless, the loss of Glo was one that I have never gotten over—and hope I never will.

DESPITE THE THOUGHTS of my beloved wife, I *still* couldn't sleep and began to recite the following verse, idiotically:

Thomas Gnu
Thomas Gnu
How shall I deal with
Thomas Gnu?

Since I was not about to enter some kind of haïku competition, I could see that continuing to recite the verse was not going to be profitable. And it certainly would not bring me any closer to a decision. So I forced myself to take a 180-degree turn and to contemplate mankind's ultimate destiny. (I know, I know, what about womankind? But I did not feel a need to observe such niceties at the moment.)

No matter how high our aspirations, wasn't each of us consigned to end up as a speck of dust? And did that not hold true for the mightiest among us—be it Microsoft's Bill Gates or the fellows who head up Disney? However significant their achievements, no matter how high their year-end grosses, their time on earth was but the blink of an eyelash in terms of eternity. With tremendous luck and good fortune, the president of the United States himself, in all his eminence, would at best qualify as a cosmic footnote.

So where on the scale of importance did that leave the likes of a worthless sack of protoplasm such as Dickie Moué?

There was, of course, a humanistic flaw in this line of reasoning—mankind will prevail, every life has worth, Hitler himself enjoyed Alice Faye movies and Bavarian meat pies—that type of thing—but I had neither the time nor the inclination to think all of that through.

Rather than continue to twirl about in indecision, I decided to take up Peabody on his proposal. My feeling was that any decision was better than none—although some of my past ones had been disastrous.

Strangely enough, it was not the money that convinced me to proceed, although clearly that was a factor. Nor was it my cosmic speculations. Much more important was having something to do, and I'm not just talking about a reason to get out of the house. You certainly don't go around killing people for that. What I meant was a real assignment that I could go right to work on rather than have to wait around for an opportunity that might never come. As an unemployed fellow of a certain age, with no future to speak of, I had begun to dry up in spirit. What good was I to myself? What kind of role model did I present to

Lettie, always going around with my heart in my throat, and making it worse with my attempts to be cheerful.

Without a function, I had ceased to feel like a man. Had I continued on the same path, I might very well have decided to join the famous socialite at the bottom of Liar's Pond.

FIRST THING IN the morning, I wasted no time in contacting Peabody at his hotel.

"Who *is* this?" he asked, his voice both hoarse and suspicious, which was quite a combination.

"William Binny."

"Oh yes," he said. "Were you at Frolique last night?"

"No, I stayed home."

"I did as well. I was tempted to go, but I'd been drinking a bit heavily and thought I'd get a good night's rest. Have you given any thought to our project?"

"Quite a bit."

"And your decision?"

"Count me in."

"That's splendid. I couldn't be more delighted. I'll make all the arrangements and then you can review them and see if they're to your liking. It's the way I prefer to work, and I hope you find it satisfactory."

"Sounds good to me."

Chapter Six

HE FOLLOWING DAY, a fat FedEx package arrived, the delivery of which was thrilling in itself, since it was the first one I had ever received. It contained an itinerary for both me and Dickie Moué, some airline tickets and a dozen or so packets that were tightly wrapped and heavy enough to contain bricks. I peeked inside one and saw that it contained crisp new hundred-dollar bills. It surprised me that Peabody's organization would entrust all that cash to the mails. But then I thought about it and realized that it was considered tip money when you were involved in a global enterprise.

Had the FedEx man known what was in there he might have bolted and had a great time for himself in Puerto Vallarta or some place like that—until they caught up with him.

I did not count the money—I'm not that way, having always felt that you either trust someone or you don't. And let's say I had been shorted a few hundred. What difference would it make in the universal scheme?

Moué's itinerary indicated that he would be arriving in Miami Beach in three days—and there was a notation saying I could either use the airline tickets or receive a cash credit if I decided to drive. There was also a reservation for the week's rental of a condo on Lincoln Road. Some photos had been included showing Dickie Moué on the deck of a yacht, which served to confirm my feelings about the man. He wore a navy blue blazer, an ascot, a captain's hat, and the sonofabitch had his arms around two half-naked homewreckers who were probably refugees from the Cannes film festival. I hated his arrogant and scornful patrician features. He represented everything that had gone wrong in America.

And it was about time someone settled his hash.

Nowhere in the various documents was there any mention

of my name. They were all made out to a fellow named Matthew T. Morning, which I assumed was to be my alias.

It was the perfect choice. The name had a quiet yet intriguing ring to it and might have belonged to a gunslinger of the Old West (Matt Morning, back then) who had retired to lead a circumspect life. Yet a fellow who was ready to strap on his guns at a moment's notice if a situation that called for it arose. I was delighted with the name and could hardly wait to try it out.

Furthermore, it strengthened my confidence in Peabody's taste and judgment.

I tore off some of the hundreds and stuck them in my jeans, just to see how it would feel—and in doing so got a little surge in my loins. Score one for Mr. Freud. Then I looked around for a place to hide the other packets—which was not as easy as it seemed. Every place I thought of—my toolbox, the cold cuts compartment of the refrigerator—seemed to cry out: "Look in here for a bunch of money!"

Finally, I put the packets inside my Capons softball team jacket, which I no longer had the heart to wear. Then I bundled it up and stuck it as far back on the closet shelf as it would go. My thought was that I would slide the money into my checking account, a few hundred at a time, so as not to throw up a flag. If you made a large deposit, the tellers in our town were not beyond making a comment, such as "mmmmm, I see somebody's rich aunt must have died."

But that is one of the disadvantages—and there aren't many—of living in a small town.

I TOLD LETTIE I'd be going out of town for a few days on a job.

"How many days?" she asked.

"Three or four."

"How come you can't tell me the exact number?"

"Because I don't know. It's open-ended."

I could tell she was not happy with that answer. To make it

up to her, I took her over to a branch of The Gap that had just opened in the new mall and told her to pick out an outfit. (What's a daughter for if you can't spoil her?)

She circled the store, checking the price tag of each item, and then moved on, assuming the garment was beyond our financial means. When I saw her do that, I got sick at heart and knew I had made the right move in accepting Peabody's offer, no matter what its nature.

"Just pick something out," I told her. "And never mind how much it costs."

"Did we get rich?"

"We got comfortable."

She selected an ensemble she had seen in Sassy magazine, which I paid for with one of the hundreds.

The saleswoman looked it over carefully.

"You could shave with one of these," she said.

"I use an electric razor," I said, in an attempt to lighten the atmosphere with a little humor.

But I could see that those fresh new hundreds might cause trouble, particularly in our close-knit community, where such signs of affluence were uncommon.

"SHE WAS IMPRESSED by those hundreds," said Lettie as we walked back to the Trooper. "My girlfriends would be, too."

"The last thing I want to do is impress anybody."

"Do you have more of those—or just the ones in your pocket?"

"We have some more," I said vaguely.

"What would happen if there was no such thing as money?" she asked, a welcome line of inquiry, since I was not anxious to pursue the subject of our personal finances.

"We would return to the barter system. If I were a plumber, I would fix your pipes. And if you were a dentist, you would fix my teeth in exchange."

75

"What if there was nothing wrong with your teeth."

"Then you would *find* something wrong with them."

THAT NIGHT, I made arrangements for Lettie and the cats to stay over at the house of her best friend, Edwina, while I was away. My daughter had assured me that although Edwina had kissed three boys, she had not made out with any of them, and that she was doing great in Social Studies. Additionally, her mother had dropped the boyfriend with the dirty fingernails and was now dating a hotel manager who took great pride in his personal appearance.

Armed with this comforting new information, I felt reasonably secure that I had placed Lettie and the cats in safe hands.

With my daughter accounted for, I waited for a call from Peabody who did not disappoint me.

"Is this the residence of Mr. Matthew T. Morning?" was his sly inquiry on the phone.

The question surprised me since up until that time I had not known him to have a satirical bent.

"It certainly is," I said, going along with the gag.

"Are the arrangements satisfactory?"

"They're just fine."

We agreed, for sentimental reasons, to meet that night at Frolique where we would tie up any loose ends.

When I arrived, he was in a shouting match with Cassie, the scrawny but hot-looking blonde who was doing the show that night, having completed her industrial-cleaning job out of town.

From what I could gather, Peabody had advised her to change her yellow sequined panties into what he felt was a more suitable color—and for good measure had thrown in some tips on how to improve her dance routine.

"I was only trying to help, darling," he said in a strangled voice.

"Well, thank you very much, Mr. *Steven* Spielberg," she said.

"There's no need to have a hissy fit."

"Piss off," she said, and flounced off to her dressing room.

"Hello, Binny," he said. "I've ordered our Stollies. And if there's one thing I've learned from this experience, it's that you mustn't criticize a woman's wardrobe."

I agreed—though I had little experience in this area.

At that point, I was unable to resist asking him if he had followed up on Mary's proposal to go to bed with him for $1,700.

"What about Mary?"

"I was prepared to pay her the money," he said. "I had it piled up on my nightstand, but she refused to take my calls."

"Amazing," I said. "For that amount of money, I would have showed up myself."

"That's very kind of you," he said, not acknowledging the jesting nature of my offer. "But I'm afraid it's the story of my life."

After a long, mournful sigh, he recovered quickly and said: "Now look here, I hope you're taking our venture seriously."

"What makes you think I'm not?"

"Don't misunderstand. I'm aware you're an honorable fellow, but you mustn't fail, Binny. I don't want to be fired. It happened to me once, and I was shattered."

"It happened to me, too."

"I was working for a bail bondsman," he said, showing no interest in my own unhappy experience. "He called me into his office, looked me right in the eye and said I was a cunt. That mustn't happen again."

"I'll try to see that it doesn't."

"Cheers," he said, apparently reassured.

We drank up and turned to look at Cassie, who had ignored Peabody's advice and did her routine exactly the way she had always done it, if not more so. I enjoyed watching her dance no matter what color her panties were. So long as the half-moons of her butt stuck out of them. I had once considered calling Cassie for a date, but she lived with an ailing hockey star who had chosen our community for retirement, and I did not want to get into the middle of that. Had I been an ailing hockey star, I would not have wanted someone fooling around with *my* girlfriend.

Peabody watched Cassie vacantly, and I could tell he still preferred the good-natured Mary, shapeless body and all.

Then he turned to me, his eyes sparkling.

"We're doing it, aren't we," he said softly.

"We sure are."

"Yes-s-s-!" he said, pumping his arm in a gesture that seemed to be mandatory for rising young television comedians. "Yes-s-s!"

Two fellows at the next table looked over at us. Though the light was dim, I recognized them as being the surly and antisocial Grimble brothers. They were electricians who had the slogan, LET US REMOVE YOUR SHORTS printed on their truck. It was amusing enough, but I wondered what it would be like to have to read the same joke every day of your life.

The Grimbles had tangled with just about everyone in the community, including Little Irwin, who had acquitted himself well, since he had the ability to get down low and keep up-ending them. Touch wood, they had not gotten around to messing with me, but I braced myself for trouble, all the same. As it turned out, the Grimbles, perhaps because it was their night out, were in a good mood. They got caught up in Peabody's enthusiasm, and before long, they were pumping their arms along with him and also calling out, "Yes-s-s-s-."

Inspired by their support, Peabody jumped up on our table and started stamping his feet, and hollering out the same jubilant cry! I got into it a little myself, although I did not jump up there with him. Soon he had the whole place going. Like a deranged master of ceremonies, he pumped and yessed his way

78

from table to table and might have continued on that way all night if the owners hadn't flashed the closing sign.

PEABODY FINALLY CALMED down as we walked across the parking lot to get the Trooper.

"Should I have asked them to join us?" he asked.

"The Grimble brothers? I don't think so. They seem decent enough, but they have hair-trigger tempers and can turn on you. For example, if you don't pay them on time, they'll come to your house and rip out the wiring."

"Well, I'm not *gay,*" he said, "If that's what you're thinking. No one has ever stuck a finger in my ass and sucked my cock."

"Who said you're gay?"

"I thought you might have suggested it."

"Uh uh. That's in your head."

"Good. Because I'm not."

He started to get into the Trooper and then stopped.

"But we're doing it, aren't we, Binny."

"I leave tomorrow."

He looked at me fondly in the moonlight.

Then he crouched down, squeezed his eyes shut, pumped his arm one more time and bellowed out a final cry.

"*YES-S-S-S!*"

Chapter Seven

THOUGH I COULD barely sleep that night for all the excitement, I got out of bed at six the next morning feeling refreshed and exuberant. There is something about starting a new job, no matter what it is. I packed a few items of clothing, including my all-purpose blue suit jacket with the gold buttons, but I did not overdo it, thinking I would pick up an outfit or two once I arrived in Miami Beach and got the lay of the land in a fashion sense. There was no point in standing out.

I keep a shotgun under lock and key for home protection, but I decided to let it stay where it was. Strictly speaking, I am not a gun person, which makes me an oddity in this area. (I do take advantage of the reduced rates offered by the Gun Club for their theatre parties. A favorite booking? You guessed it. *Annie Get Your Gun.*)

Still, I have seen the mayhem such weapons can cause and don't care to keep a bunch of them around. I did take along a Navajo scrimshaw knife, one of my prized possessions. After seeing it in the window of a men's shop in Chicago, I had circled the store half a dozen times before deciding to bite the bullet and purchase it, despite the exorbitant price.

It's really a beauty, not that I ever thought it would be of any practical value. Little Irwin had once cautioned me against producing a knife in a fight—unless I planned to use it.

"Otherwise," he said, "you will find it stuck up your ass."

Thus far, I had heeded his advice.

How I missed that horny little hell-raiser!

As for a disguise, I was already *in* one in a sense—since no one other than friends and family could ever remember what I looked like. Medium height, medium build, medium everything. But instead of wearing my hair in the usual modified comb-over, I tried slicking it straight back and was shocked by

83

what I saw in the mirror. It was like getting an accidental look at your own butt. My face seemed naked, but I decided to let it stay that way, since the new hairstyle really did alter my appearance.

After gassing up the Trooper, I hit the highway, experiencing that sense of possibility and rejuvenation that millions had felt before me. I am not the first to note that it is a uniquely American phenomenon. I'm sure that the Japanese, too, to cite an example, enjoy getting out on the road. But I cannot imagine them doing it with as much gusto. Possibly because the minute they get out there and start enjoying themselves, they run out of road. (And I say this without gloating. It is just an accident of their unfortunate geography.)

I cut across country and made it to north Florida in eight hours flat. It was a smooth trip up to that point, except for a fellow with a BOYCOTT VEAL bumper sticker who tried to run me off the road. (And I don't even eat much veal.) After I hit Jacksonville, I thought to myself that's it, Binny. You are home free. Check into a cozy little Comfort Inn, have a good night's sleep and then waltz into Miami Beach the next morning, ready to do battle. But I had miscalculated the size of Florida, which does not seem like all that much on the map, but in actuality goes on forever. You could fit a dozen Israels in it and have room left over to spare.

I floored it at that point since Dickie Moué had already been in Miami Beach for twenty-four hours and would be leaving in two days more for the Caribbean islands.

By nightfall of the following day, I noticed that the music on the car radio had segued over from heartsick country ballads to catchy Latino orchestrations, signaling that I was nearing my destination. But I could not fully enjoy the music since a driving rain had started up, and I could barely make out the highway signs. (So much for their vaunted perfect weather.)

Each time I thought I was in Miami Beach I went sweeping off on to some freeway and ended up in places like Grapeland Heights and Key Biscayne. I got so frustrated that I pulled over to the side and just sat there, thinking of what it would be like if I never got there and had to return all that money to Peabody. To top it off, my wipers had gotten jammed. It was one of those days.

I got out of the car to see if I could get them going again and saw a yellow Cadillac pull up behind me with a gray-haired oldtimer behind the wheel. Ignoring the rain, he got out of the car and approached me, having obviously sympathized with my situation. He wore a baseball cap, a jogging suit and sneakers with the laces untied. Yet, despite his get-up, he did not strike me as being the athletic type.

"What's the matter?" he asked. "You lost or something?"

"I've been trying to find Miami Beach, but I keep sliding past it. Basically, I'm lost."

"What do you mean 'basically'? You're either lost or you're not."

"I guess I'm lost."

"You *guess* you're lost? What is this, a guessing game? With prizes? Maybe we should get a sponsor."

"I'm *lost* goddamit."

"All right, don't get excited. *You* get excited, then *I'll* get excited and next thing you know we'll be rolling around on the ground and slugging it out. I did that once with my brother, and I ended up with a back condition. And you and I don't even know each other. So calm down. Now that we got it straightened out that you're lost—and believe me, it wasn't easy—maybe I can help you. You look like a nice man, and we don't want you to go home with a bad impression because then you'll never come back, and frankly, we need the money. I'd ask you to come for dinner, but if you tasted my wife's cooking, then you'd *really* have a problem, and you're in enough trouble already."

He seemed to be putting on a little show for me, and if it wasn't for the driving rain and my situation, I would have found it most enjoyable.

Still, I could not restrain my curiosity about him.

"Are you a comedian?" I asked.

"Are you crazy? If I was a comedian why would I be standing out here in the rain talking to a perfect stranger? What's so funny about that?"

"Why not just point me toward the highway."

"*Point* you toward it? What good is that gonna do? Are you gonna sit here and study it? I'll do something even better. Follow me and I'll show you exactly where you wanna go."

True to his word, he got back in the Cadillac and led me to the correct turnoff. Then he waved through the window and did not even stop for a thank-you.

By this time, I had identified his humor as being of the Borscht Belt variety, which is generally not to my liking. But his was an exception. And I certainly did appreciate his help.

If he wasn't a good Samaritan, I'd like to know who is. (And by the way, is there any such thing as a *bad* Samaritan? Someone should check that out. For all I know, I might even *be* one.)

I FOUND MY condo/hotel easily enough. Much like Peabody's office building, it was a spare and chilly-looking structure that had a global feel to it. I could still smell the plaster drying, which led me to believe it had just been built. The lobby was empty except for an Hispanic fellow who took a glance at my reservation form and said: "Just follow me, Señor Morning."

Hearing my alias pronounced aloud gave me a little jiggle since it was the first time it had been put to use. (I believe the French call it a *frisson.*) I followed the fellow up in the elevator to an apartment on the twelfth floor. He handed me the key and left without a word, leading me to believe that he had been trained to say and do as little as possible. Like myself, he was probably a small player in a global network, and might not even have known that he was.

The apartment, as I had imagined it would be, was sparsely

furnished, but it had a terrace with a sweeping view of a canal and what I took to be the skyline of Miami itself. You could see planes twinkling in to the airport, no doubt carrying shipments of drugs from South America, to further sap our nation's vitality. A single look at the map is all it takes to see that it is impossible to stop the flow, and that our only hope is to get at the root cause of this craving for noxious substances. Yet obviously, there are bigwigs with a need to see this traffic continue. (I just wonder why!)

Still, the view was magnificent, although I was so exhausted that I could not really drink it in.

I unpacked and got into a shortic nightgown, one of a three-pak that Glo, God rest her soul, had picked out for me at the Wal-Mart. She would always buy as many as a dozen items when one would do—no doubt a result of her being from a military family that had to move around a lot—with all the attendant insecurity. It was financially ruinous for us, but I put up with it, since, in Glo's case, the good far outweighed the bad. On one occasion, I retired our credit card, but quickly applied for reinstatement since I could not bear to witness her silent grief.

I looked around for something to read. No matter how tired I am, I always try to get in a chapter or two before retiring. It works like a sleeping pill. Since I had not brought along any reading material, I picked up one of the half-dozen volumes that were displayed on the bookshelf, probably for show. It was called, *Investing in Cold Blood* and the flap said it had to do with leaving your emotions behind when you set out to make money. It was written by a fellow with a Ph.D. who claimed to have done that and gotten rich (as a young fellow he had invested *emotionally* and lost his shirt).

I riffled through a few pages to see if it would hold my interest and came across a piece of a memorandum that had been used as a bookmark and had probably been left in there by accident. Possibly by the previous operative. (Dreams of glory! I had started to think of myself as an 'operative.')

At the top, where it was torn, it said . . . "tremely confidential. For your eyes only."

Once again, I got a shivery feeling. It was my first Confidential Memo. From what I could gather, it was part of a prospectus letter to a select group of investors, offering them a chance to get in on the takeover of a tool-and-die company in Switzerland and promising them the "usual" return of 315 percent over a period of four years. The plan was immediately to fire a few thousand people and make it a leaner operation. And there was a note indicating that US regulatory statutes did not apply.

It certainly beat the four percent return on my CD, and I made a note to ask Peabody, in a roundabout way, if a fellow like myself could get in on something like that.

After all, I *was* a global player, albeit a minor one.

In case I had any doubts about being in the big leagues, the memo put an end to them. I slipped it back in the book—in case someone came back for it. Then I got into bed and amazed myself by falling asleep immediately.

It may not have been the sleep of the just, but it was good enough for me.

Up and at 'em, big guy, I said to myself, as I opened my eyes the next morning. It's time to get serious.

The sunlight came streaming in through the terrace door, which I took to be a hopeful sign.

I got out of bed and did a variety of warmup exercises that I had picked up over the years, some for strength, others for circulation, and a few I had seen on the O.J. Simpson workout tape. Say what you will about the controversial (and some might add guilty-as-sin) gridiron star, his fitness tape is excellent. So he had done some good in that area.

Despite the dark nature of my assignment, I saw no reason not to kick off the day by eating a substantial breakfast. With that purpose in mind, I set off down the street and soon found a crowded little Jewish deli that looked inviting.

The customers represented what I took to be a cross section of Miami Beach society—little old ladies in all their finery, Cuban gentlemen bent over rice and beans, a gathering of bearded Hasidic fellows and right alongside them, some girls who looked like models, each one a stringbean and a heartbreaker. Sitting around the biggest table was a contingent of broad-boned military-slick police officers, each one with a small cannon sticking out of his holster. Crouched over their plates, they surrounded their food with beefy forearms, looking up warily from time to time, as if someone was going to snatch it away. If I had to guess, I'd say their breakfasts were on the house.

Oddly enough, their presence made me feel secure, which was ridiculous when you consider the purpose of my visit to Miami.

There was only one waiter for the whole restaurant, a fellow with sparse red hair who wore a flowered shirt and khaki shorts and Reebok sneakers. I can't say why—it was just a feeling I had—but he came off as being a little on the gay side. If so, he was of the quick-tempered variety that you do not mess around with. (I should point out that I am a little afraid of gay people in general—and I don't have to be told that it has to do with various insecurities of my own. I *know* that and would prefer not to go into it right now.)

I noticed that the waiter—who may or may not have been gay—got snappish whenever a customer was indecisive about his order. So I made sure mine was ready when he showed up. It was coffee and corned beef hash with fried eggs set out on top of it, designed to drip down onto the hash. But sure enough, I was slow in making up my mind about what type of juice to order—and got a groan and a roll of the eyes from the waiter in return.

To his credit, he called the ninety-year-old ladies "girls" ("Some more coffee, girls?"), which I thought was a nice touch. Too often, old-timers are treated rudely in our society. (I feel this is *our* loss as much as theirs.)

All in all, the deli was a far cry from the Edward Bivens diner with its complement of bland statehouse types.

After polishing off my hash, which was superior, I paid the check and asked the proprietor for directions to the Bancroft Hotel. He said it was within walking distance and showed me how to get there.

"I catered a party there last month and I'm still waiting to get paid. They're nice people until you try to get a quarter out of them. Then, all of a sudden, they don't know you.

"Maybe you can pick up a few dollars for me while you're over there. I can't give you a commission, but next time you come in, I'll seat you at a lovely table and make sure the eggs are fresh. I personally don't like an egg to be fresh to me, but that's *my* problem."

I responded with a chuckle and noted that everywhere you turned in Miami Beach, there was a comedian in your face. It occurred to me that I had never met a Jewish individual who did not have a comical side. (Abner Teitlebaum being the one exception, which should have thrown up a flag.) No doubt this arises from their troubled past. When faced with history's indignities, what choice did they have but to laugh or cry. They had chosen the former, and I was with them all the way. In that sense, aren't we all Jews? (But maybe that's a reach.)

I found the Bancroft Hotel in short order, and what a little treasure it turned out to be. It had a quiet kind of luxurious atmosphere that did not hit you over the head, a style that I had never known and probably never would. The walls in the lobby were constructed of rich antique wood and the corner moldings had little Greek mythology-style cupids attached to them. There were groupings of fresh flowers set out on tables that stood on little curved legs. It reminded me of the old hotel I had stayed at on my trip to the Republic of Czechoslovakia. If anything, the Bancroft seemed more authentic, as if it had been picked up whole and shipped over from the Old Country.

Never mind the rooms—I could picture me and Lettie moving right into the lobby.

On a more somber note, there were security guards all over the place, stationed ten feet apart, each one a well-built dark-complected fellow in a business suit with a walkie-talkie in his pocket and a cord leading up to his ear. The Bancroft was probably the most secure establishment I had ever come across (with the possible exception of our topless bar, Frolique), which is no doubt one of the reasons why Dickie Moué and the other well-heeled residents had elected to stay there. Yet for all of the security I was able, amazingly, to sail right through the lobby to the desk of the concierge without drawing so much as a suspicious glance. So clearly I did not fit the profile of the type of fellow they would want to frisk or fling to the ground. To the contrary, decked out as I was in my all-purpose blue suit jacket, freshly pressed jeans and white sneakers (and don't forget, my sparse hair was slicked back in a Fred Astaire Roaring Twenties style), I probably came across as a preppy-type fellow who fit right in with the clientele. (The possibility existed, of course, that I was secretly being clocked—and they were not letting on. But that is probably my paranoid side at work.)

The concierge was a gray-haired fellow in a green uniform with epaulettes—who wore pince-nez and had his own desk, way over in the corner.

To show that I was not in awe of my surroundings, I deliberately affected a high-blown manner of speaking.

"I wonder if you would assist me," I said. "I'd like to know the whereabouts of Dickie Moué."

"Of course, sir. Mr. Dickie Moué is one of our most valued and honored guests and returns to us year after year. Those of us on the staff feel privileged to be able to serve him—who shall I say is calling?''

"Bill Binny," I said, completely forgetting my alias.

It was a blunder, but perhaps understandable considering I had never addressed a concierge before and that I had, after all, been Bill Binny all my life.

"What I mean to say," I added, in an attempt to recover, "is that I'm Matthew T. Morning. Bill Binny is an associate of mine. We work so closely that sometimes I forget who's who."

"Of course," he said, narrowing his eyes slightly, but only for an instant. "To my recollection, Mr. Dickie Moué and his lovely wife, Ilyana, are reclining on the terrace, as is their custom after breakfast. May I have the honor of announcing you?"

"That won't be necessary," I said. "I'm an old friend of the Moués and would prefer to surprise them."

"As you wish, sir. It was my pleasure to serve you. Feel free to contact me if you find yourself in need of further assistance."

He bowed and then stood up triumphantly as if he'd presented me with a prize, when all he had done really was to pass along a piece of simple information. I could just about imagine how he would carry on if I'd asked him something more complicated—like how do you rent a boat. Then I realized he was looking for a tip and handed him a crisp five.

"No, no," he said, throwing up his arms and recoiling as if I had offered him a snake. "I couldn't possibly."

"I insist," I said.

"Very well then," he said, snatching the five out of my hand and putting it in his pocket. "But I assure you, it's not necessary. My sole interest is to serve."

I crossed the lobby and followed the signs to the outdoor patio, sliding past another contingent of security guards who showed even less interest in me than the first bunch. At least outwardly. As I stepped out onto the crowded patio, I got hit by a babble of foreign tongues. It was as if I had walked onto the floor of the United Nations. I felt like I was the only American out there, which was not surprising. How many of us could afford such unbridled luxury! I counted three swimming pools, each one oblong shaped and with its own decorative individually designed waterfall.

I took a seat at a little counter bar over on the side and ordered a tropical drink, telling the cocktail waitress to go easy on the rum, since obviously I needed to keep a clear head. She was a nice-looking redhead who wore a halter top and bluejean cutoffs and spoke with a Texas accent. I felt better knowing there were at least two of us who were Americans.

The women around the pool, regardless of age, all wore thong bikinis, many of them going topless, no matter what kind of shape they were in. I am no stranger to the naked female form in all its contortions, having made my small contribution to the billion-dollar-a-year video porn industry. But there is something about a normal everyday woman baring her breasts in a public situation that gets to me. One of the guests, a middle-aged blonde with a good figure—who for all I know may have been a mother—excused herself from her international party and walked over to a secluded corner of the patio to adjust her thong; from what I could see, she was trying to get it to go even deeper up her butt. I wasn't sure how I felt about that. It had been deep enough for me to begin with. But maybe if I had asked for some more rum in my tropical drink, I would have appreciated what she was trying to achieve a bit more.

I asked the cocktail waitress if she could do me a favor and point out Dickie Moué. She must have been new at the job, and whenever she didn't know the answer to something—or couldn't find some item behind the bar—she would put her hands to her cheeks and say, "Oh Lordy." She did that when I asked her about Dickie Moué, but then something in her head must have clicked; she nodded toward a couple at the far end of the patio who had their backs turned to the other guests and appeared to be staring soulfully out at the distant ocean. The woman was tall and slim and wore a straw hat and a white linen dress. The man beside her was in a navy blue blazer and white slacks and wore a paisley ascot around his neck. He was in a wheelchair.

"Are you sure that's Dickie Moué?" I asked.

"That's him, bless his poor soul."

Trying not to be conspicuous, I moved closer to the couple and saw that the man in the wheelchair was indeed the fellow that I had come looking for—although he was at least sixty pounds heavier than he appeared to be in Peabody's photographs. Not only that, but even though he continued to look rakish and arrogant, one of his eyes was unfocused and his hands shook.

Despite his unhappy state, he seemed much too young to have been a classmate of the elderly Thomas Gnu, unless, of course, his condition had ironically thrown the aging process into reverse.

Whatever the case, I cannot tell you how upset and disappointed I was by this new development. It was one thing to go after some uncaring Ivy Leaguer who was enriching himself at the expense of the little fellow—and quite another to deal with a helpless fat guy in a wheelchair. It brought down the whole experience, and I was pissed off at Peabody to say the least. Surely with the resources at his command, he had been updated on Dickie Moué's plight; yet he had callously sent me after him all the same. All of this so disturbed me that I paid for my drink and took off. There was no way I was going to keep up my end of the deal. If it meant I would have to return my advance, so be it.

I'd find some other way for me and Lettie to get by.

ODDLY ENOUGH, NOW that I had changed direction and was relatively innocent of mind and heart, several of the security guards eyed me suspiciously as I approached the front door of the hotel.

One of them stepped out in front of me and stood there, arms folded, legs spread apart—a position he had no doubt paid a lot of money to learn in some fly-by-night security school.

"May I help you, signor?" he asked.

"Not just now," I said with a friendly smile.

He looked me over for what seemed like an hour and a half during which time it crossed my mind that Dickie Moué had been tipped off to my arrival and the purpose of my visit. But even if Peabody (and who else could it be?) had been capable of such treachery—which I seriously doubted—what good would it do either of us?

Fortunately, my suspicions proved to be unfounded.

"Forgive me, signor," said the guard. "We're looking for a certain type."

"I don't blame you," I said. (The guard then stepped aside, allowing me to return to my condo/hotel without further incident.)

The first thing I did was to put a call through to Peabody. I was determined to read him the riot act. But the clerk at his hotel said he had checked out.

"Did he leave a forwarding number?"

"I'm afraid not."

Words cannot describe how shaken I was when I hung up. Let me amend that. Words can describe anything if you know how to use them properly—which I was too upset to do. Why would Peabody disappear on me like that? I felt hurt and abandoned, much the same as I had when my mother took off with one of her lending-library browsers. There is probably a connection between the two desertions if you buy into the whole psychological mindset, which I admit I do now and then.

Had Peabody set me up? Let's say I had gone ahead with the transaction and gotten caught. And after excruciating pressure had been brought to bear on me, I buckled and told the authorities I had been innocently drawn into the plot by a certain Valentine Peabody. (I would have resisted strongly, of course, but who among us can define exactly what our breaking point is?) Still, what if I had been forced to tell them about Valentine Peabody and there was no such person to be found? What if he had cleared out his office, leaving no evidence that there ever *was* a Valentine Peabody? Ed Bivens could vouch for his existence, but with that detached style of his, you never knew which way he would turn.

It's true I had the advance, but I had done nothing to earn it and did not feel it was rightfully mine. There is no record of thievery in my past (one of the reasons, no doubt, that Peabody had picked me out). Knowing my nature, I would probably try to figure out a way to return the money. Unless I went ahead and killed Dickie Moué on my own, a course I had already abandoned.

Seduced and betrayed. Those are the words that fit my situation. And then the phone rang and who should the caller be but none other than Valentine Peabody.

"Hello, Binny. Peabody here. I understand you've been trying to reach me."

"I certainly have." I said, marveling at how quickly he had heard about my call.

Was nothing beyond the reach of these global people!

"I'm here in Karachi. There was no point in hanging about while you were working, so I thought I'd pop over here for a bit. My daughter, Millie, is appearing in *Guys and Dolls* and she was anxious for me to see her perform."

"They do *Guys and Dolls* in Karachi?" I said, caught off stride for the moment.

"Oh, yes. It's performed in Urdu, but quite surprisingly, a good deal of the flavor comes through. She's playing Nathan Detroit. I'm sure you remember the role."

As if to refresh my memory, he began to sing the celebrated verse about Good Old Reliable Nathan, belting it out in a raucous British music-hall style and enjoying every second of it.

"My daughter *likes Guys and Dolls,*" I shouted, cutting him off, and aware that I was still, obviously, sidetracked.

"That's lovely. Perhaps she and Millie can perform a duet. How's it coming along?"

"Not that great. You didn't tell me what kind of shape the poor man was in."

"Dickie? Oh, yes, I suppose I should have mentioned that and you have my apologies. But you musn't let it throw you off. I've been through this before—you're new at it, you must remember—and there's always *something* that doesn't go quite right, generally when you're halfway along. The tendency is to throw up one's hands and be done with it—and I can assure you, it's a mistake. The trick is to keep your eye on the ultimate goal."

"How am I supposed to kill a helpless fellow in a wheelchair?"

"He's still a *pig,* isn't he? And besides, he's much closer to his maker now than ever. You'd be doing the bastard a favor. Now be a good fellow—I know it's hard—but grit your teeth and go back to work. You'll feel much better in the end. And God knows, you don't want to return all that lovely money. Lettie is going to want things.

"Believe me, I have experience with my own daughters."

"She wants things already," I conceded.

"Then there you are. And it's only going to get worse, trust me on that. Just this morning, I had to lay out five thousand dollars for a computer workstation, and I'm sure it's just *one* of Millie's whims. I insisted that she contribute a thousand out of her trust fund, but all the same . . . Now off you go, Binny."

"I'm not sure I can pull this off."

"Nonsense. I have every confidence that you can. And it will be well worth it. Oh . . . one more thing."

"What's that?"

"I miss you."

"Me too," I said automatically.

And then we both hung up.

THE ODDEST THING is that I did miss the fucker. The silky voice, the suave confidence, the English accent with a little Karachi thrown in. Ed Bivens had been right on the money when he said I needed a Continental individual in my life. Not to speak of a brand-new friend. And what a friend he was! If it was true that we had entered the global decade, Valentine Peabody represented my last chance to get on-line.

I had missed him and now I had him back.

To top it all off, he had made some sense. What difference did it make that Dickie Moué wasn't feeling that hot? Wasn't he the same sonofabitch he had always been? For all I knew, he was ordering factory layoffs from his wheelchair. Had Adolf Hitler, the very personification of evil in our time, undergone a transformation during his last days in the bunker?

As Lettie would say: *hardly!*

And he was right about my daughter, too. It made me uncomfortable each time he worked her into the equation—as if he was an old family friend—but God knows, she was after me for material possessions every twenty minutes; and I was not the type of father who could say forget it, go do the dishes.

I shuddered to think what would happen when she entered her crazy teens.

So I decided to honor my commitment after all—to return to the Bancroft and see if I could get Dickie Moué alone somehow. Then do the deed quickly, drive back home and put the whole episode behind me.

There were times when I wished I was one of those ice-cold killers who acts without remorse. But to a great extent, I remained a caring individual and would have to work with what I had.

Now that I had become a familiar face (and was back on a

deadly track), several of the security guards greeted me with a friendly nod, one of them flashing a toothy Latino grin.

Where do they *find* these people!

The concierge hailed my arrival as if I was the hotel's favorite visitor.

"Good morning, Mr. Morning," he said, "so nice to see you again. I hope you don't mind my putting the two "Mornings" together. Many of our guests enjoy a little pleasanterie as a relief from the harsh realities of the workaday world."

"I know what they mean," I said, marveling at what five bucks could get you at the Bancroft.

"Mr. Dickie Moué and his lovely wife have retired to their suite. Shall I ring them and tell them you are on the premises?"

"I don't think so," I said. "I'm just going to take a little stroll around."

"Excellent. Is there some way that I can be of service?"

"Not just now."

"Very well then," he said, quickly dropping his eyes and shuffling some papers.

He had obviously been looking for another five, but I didn't want to get into the habit of laying one on him every time I passed his desk.

I walked to the end of the lobby and stopped at a guest directory, which was fastened to the wall. It had each of the tenants' names listed on a separate brass plaque—like a war memorial. At the end of a long strip of German and Japanese names, I found one for D. Moué, on the fourteenth floor.

In keeping with the hotel's Old World style, the elevator had a lot of grandeur to it, but the ride upstairs was slow and shaky. I finally reached the fourteenth floor and stepped out into the corridor, which was carpeted and quiet as a tomb. As I strolled past Dickie Moué's suite, I noticed that although the service entrance door was closed, the one at the main entrance was open a few inches.

In my boldest move thus far, I pushed it open a bit more

and caught a glimpse of Moué sitting on the terrace. (If they caught me, I was prepared to say that I was thinking of renting a similar suite on the floor below, and must have gotten mixed up. And they would probably drop it at that.) Dickie wore a smoking jacket and was puffing on a thin cigar, staring out at the sea. It occurred to me that I could just slip in there, lift the wheeler and tip him over the railing. When I first broke into poultry, I had been assigned to the assembly and servicing of incubators, a task that had resulted in my developing powerful arms. I am also the one who splits logs for our home heating. So it would not have been difficult for me to lift him up and over and send him on his way. It would appear to be a suicide, and one with obvious cause, considering the sorry shape he was in. But the plan would only work if he was alone, which I soon saw that he wasn't.

Ilyana came into view, wearing only high heels, lacy black panties and a bra. She stopped at the terrace entrance and called out to him.

"Oh, Dickie. Time for your treat."

When he turned his head toward her, she put one hand behind her head, another on her crotch, licked her lips and did a little hip-swinging hootchie-cooch dance.

Who would ever have suspected that the cool and elegant woman I had seen on the porch was capable of such shenanigans. You just never knew.

"I love it," said Dickie.

It came as a relief for me to learn that Dickie could still speak, even if it was only in short bursts.

"It's great, isn't it," said Ilyana, who seemed to be enjoying her performance as much as Dickie did.

As I looked on, the thought crossed my mind that the door had been left open deliberately—and that's how the Moué's got their jollies, letting other guests peep in on them.

But I felt I had been there long enough and taken enough chances.

So I tiptoed down the hall and returned to the tastefully decorated sitting area that had been provided for the guests while they waited for the sluggish elevator to make its tortuous way up to their floor. Taking a seat in an overstuffed chair, I picked up one of the magazines that had been thoughtfully supplied by the management. As luck would have it, the feature article dealt with the unpredictability of the prostate gland, and after reading a few paragraphs, I saw that it tied in nicely with my theory of the role of the prostate gland in historical decision-making. Such leaders as the French general Joseph Gallieni and our own Ulysses S. Grant, for example, had suffered from this painful malady and often made questionable decisions because it had kicked up on them. Had the top British naval commander in the Revolutionary War—I forget his name—not had to be shipped back to London for treatment of his prostate woes, we might still be a colony today—and not a mighty nation. The author of the article did not have the advantage of knowing about any of that, but he did have a breezy style, and I was enjoying the article thoroughly when I became aware that the Moués had joined me on the landing.

Ilyana wore another one of her cool and elegant dresses, and you would never have guessed that only a short while before she had been parading around in her undies doing scorching hot dances for her unfortunate husband. She pressed the down button, saw that the elevator had settled in on the seventh floor and sighed.

"They said they would fix this at the meeting."

"They say a lot of things, Yannie."

The elevator arrived some five minutes later, carrying a single passenger, a tiny, well-dressed woman wearing a broad-brimmed flowered hat. She had an outsized bosom and skinny little legs, but she surprised me by giving me a flirty look as I held the door for the Moués and then got in behind them.

"Ready for the long journey, everyone?" she said. "I hope you've packed a lunch."

Then she gave me another one of her flirty looks, which I felt more than compensated for her advanced age and skinny little legs.

"If they don't computerize," said Ilyana huffily, "Dickie and I are out of here."

The elevator descended slowly, almost stopped a few times, sped up erratically and then came to a complete halt just as we passed the second floor.

The door opened, leaving a crawl space about two feet high.

"Shit," said Ilyana, stamping her foot. "I *knew* this would happen."

"Amazing we got this far," said the little old lady. "I'm really impressed."

In an effort to be helpful, I rang the emergency buzzer. Soon after, several of the security guards appeared on the landing just above us.

One of them got down on his belly and reached his arms into the elevator.

"Grab ahold and I'll get you out."

"I'll be the guinea pig," said the little old lady, turning toward me.

I liked her attitude. If I ever took an ocean voyage, she is the type of person I would like to have along. And who cares what the other passengers might think about the dramatic difference in our ages.

I put my arms around her, lifting her up toward the fellow's arms, then took hold of her legs in order to shove her up there.

"Ummmm . . . nice," she said, as I hoisted her onto the landing.

What a rascal she must have been as a young girl—and still was, for my money.

Ilyana was next. She looked at me warily and with some reluctance, allowed me to help her. She was a bit heavier, and I had to first get a good grip on her thighs and then push my face against her soft perfumed butt in order to lift her properly.

"Stop that," she said, slapping back at me.

"I'm just trying to help," I said.

"I'm sure you are," she said sarcastically as the security man pulled her free.

It was Dickie Moué's turn next, and he was more of a challenge, due to all the weight he had put on. Still, I got under his huge rich-guy butt and did the best I could. It crossed my mind that if the elevator began to move upward, it would solve my problem. He would be squooshed, and I would be home free. But I had no such luck and with one last heave I was able to get him out of there.

The security guard yanked me through the open passage, thus signaling the end of the episode.

AT THAT POINT, I had to remind myself to be patient and not just charge up to Dickie Moué in public—like some political nut— just to get it over with. All that would do is get me seized by the authorities. I have a tendency to act impulsively; as an illustration, I once wrecked a hatchery when I learned that it did not, as promised, accurately duplicate the natural conditions produced by a sitting hen. I paid for the damage out of my own wages, but felt I had made my point.

Of course I was a much younger man then and have since learned to keep my emotions in check.

It was important to bide my time and see if I could get Dickie Moué when he was off by himself. He did a lot of hopeless staring out at the sea. With luck, he would want to do some of that alone, and I would have my chance.

I had had my fill of the elevator's Old World charm and took the long spiral staircase to the lobby. The concierge greeted me with a thin-lipped smile, making me feel it might have been a mistake not to have given him the other five, even though he had done absolutely nothing to earn it. I gave him a little nod as I walked past his desk and continued along until I came to a glassed-in bulletin board that posted the day's events. It listed a conference for visiting urologists, another one for Christian Coalition Florists and a third that was of special interest to me.

FRIENDS OF DICKIE MOUÉ

COCKTAIL RECEPTION

6 P.M. ABRACADABRA ROOM

Obviously, I was no friend of Dickie Moué, but I decided to pop in all the same, get lost in the crowd and see what developed. At some point in the proceedings, he might feel a need to get away from all the fawning types and wheel himself outside for some fresh air.

That would afford me a chance to take care of business and be on my way.

Clearly it was important that I be dressed in the proper attire. With that in mind, I looked for a clothing store and found a promising one nearby that featured items in the window for both sexes.

There was only one salesperson for the whole store, a young bald girl who wore a black leather halter and matching pants that were so tight you could see the outlines of her vagina, whether you wanted to or not. I have had enough experience in life to know that an outfit like that does not necessarily connote sexiness. Very often, it is quite the opposite, and it is the quiet ones who do not wear pants showing the outlines of their vaginas who are secretly hot. When I described the type of cocktail party I had been invited to, she pulled a pink madras jacket off the rack and handed it to me with two fingers as if she was doing me a favor. I wondered why the owners would want to have such a snotty salesperson in their store, unless, of course, it was difficult to get good help in Miami Beach. Or who knows, maybe most of the customers were snotty themselves and felt more comfortable having a snotty salesperson wait on them.

I tried on the pink madras jacket and felt it fit decently enough, but she insisted that the sleeves would have to be altered.

"I don't have time for that," I said. "And besides," I added, stretching the truth a bit, "I have always worn my sleeves on the long side."

When she heard that, she gave me another one of her looks and flounced off to the cash register.

In spite of her attitude, I picked out a few other items and brought them over to the sales desk. To see if I could get a rise out of her, I complimented her on her dimple.

"It's not authentic," she said. "It was chiseled out of me by a mugger in Indianapolis."

"I'm sorry to hear that," I said, in response to what appeared to be a conversation stopper.

But when I paid for my purchases in hundreds, she perked up a little—perhaps in response to the big bills. She said she had come to Miami Beach from Santa Cruz in order to pursue a modeling career, but thus far she had only landed one audition, which was for a toothpaste commercial. As yet, they had not called her back because of a division in the agency over whether to go with a bald person, no matter how good she looked otherwise. One side felt it would detract from her teeth while another faction—comprised of young guys—was willing to take its chances.

In the meanwhile she had been dating an Arab who spit at her.

"Just once," I asked, "or all the time?"

"When he's annoyed," she said. "Do you think I ought to stay with him?"

I told her I didn't see any basis there for a long-standing relationship, adding quickly that I was not anti-Arab. I wasn't pro-Arab either. I just hadn't given the Arabs much thought.

Speaking in her friend's defense, I suggested he might be from a tribe in which it's a custom to spit at their loved ones when they get excited.

"Mahmoud isn't from a tribe," she said. "He's from Chicago."

Normally, I don't like to give advice on personal affairs. There are usually two sides to any story, and for all I knew the Arab might have some serious complaints about *her*—not that I wanted to track him down and find out what they were. But this situation seemed clear-cut, so I made an exception.

"I'd get out of it."

"My thinking, too," she said with a sigh.

Though the timing was awkward, I thought about asking her out for a drink and felt she would be receptive, particularly because of her difficulties with the Arab. But I had not dated anyone since my tragic loss and wasn't sure I wanted to get off the ground with a bald salesperson. Also, I could not for the life of me figure out if she was attractive.

What, for example, would you do about the bald head? Just lick it, I imagine, and hope for the best.

Still, she was a basically aloof person, and I decided it would be a mistake to try to get something going with her. Not at that moment in time. I could just see myself being stopped in a getaway car and trying to explain away an aloof bald-headed person in the passenger seat.

But I took her number—just to be on the safe side.

To KILL SOME time before the Moué cocktail party, I walked over to the Inter-Coastal for a look at the luxury boats, some of them as big as battleships; I half expected Peabody to stroll out on the deck of one, which, of course, was unlikely. Then I gave some thought to the people who owned these boats and wondered if they were happy all the time—or did they get tired of running down to the Dry Tortugas every twenty minutes.

At one time, I would not have even permitted myself to even *think* about boats like that, but I was playing in a different league now where anything was possible. Look at how far I'd come already. If I did a great job, maybe Peabody's organization would start me off with a little twenty-footer—as a bonus.

I could just see Lettie's face when I told her it was ours.

It seems like everything I did was to see her face.

Predictably, my old friends, the security guards, waved me right through to the Moué reception. There were about fifty or sixty people gathered together in the Abracadabra Room, and I saw quickly that the pink madras jacket was a mistake since most of the fellows were wearing dark suits and ties. Maybe I would have fit right in at one of the bald saleswoman's parties, but not at this one.

Since it was too late to go back and change into my all-purpose navy blue suit jacket, I decided to stay put and take my chances.

As I passed through the rope, Ilyana gave me a suspicious look, no doubt because I had recently had my face in her butt. But she quickly became distracted by her guests who were crowded around her, telling her how fabulous she looked and, for that matter, how wonderful Dickie Moué looked, too.

"Cover of Men's Health," he said waspishly, showing he was on to them.

You had to admire him for that.

The other guests were busy telling each other where they had just come back from—and where they were going—as if it was a sin to be where they actually were. They also made promises to get together soon, which struck me as being peculiar since they already *were* together. Some waiters twirled by holding trays of canapés, which I loaded up on, thinking I might as well save on money for dinner—and forgetting that money was not my problem at the moment.

Since I saw no way at the moment to get Dickie off alone, I sat down at the bar area and listened to a piano player named Ralph play some old standards. He was remarkable in that no sooner had I thought of an old favorite, such as "Misty," then he would break out into it, as if he had been reading my mind. If Ralph wasn't famous, he should have been, and I planned to talk him up when I got home. I was so impressed with his piano playing that I folded up a five and stuck it in the little fishbowl he had next to him, after first holding it up and winking at him so that he could see that I was the one who had put it in there.

Then I sat back down and was soon joined by a florid-faced man in his sixties. He was powerfully built and had a bald head with fringes on the side in the style of a wild symphony conductor. (Glo and I used to call it the "Shostakovich look.")

He wore a plaid jacket, which made him the only other fellow at the reception who didn't fit in. That may have been why he joined me.

We both sat there in silence and listened to Ralph play "The Way You Look Tonight," which I had been about to request when he broke out into it.

"Something, isn't he," said the fellow beside me.

"I could listen to him all night," I said, knowing full well that under the circumstances, I couldn't.

"Irv Gallagher," he said, extending a huge friendly hand. "Half Yid, half Mick. Retired homicide."

I was not prepared for the ethnic slurs and must have flinched when I heard them. Nor did I feel there was any room for that kind of divisive talk in nineties' America. We've come too far for that.

He must have taken note of my reaction and chucked me lightly on the shoulder.

"No offense," he said. "It's all right when it comes from one's own."

Somewhat mollified, though not entirely, I shook his hand.

"Matthew T. Morning. Retired poultry."

"As if guys like us ever retire," he said with a wink.

"I hear you," I said, less than thrilled that he hadn't entirely given up his old profession.

"You know Dickie long?"

"Long enough," I said vaguely, as if to indicate that knowing Dickie at all was as good as knowing him for a lifetime.

But I should have known better than to try that on a retired homicide dick.

"Well, just how long *have* you known him?" he asked, squinting at me as if he had turned up a suspect, when to the best of my knowledge no crime had been committed as yet.

"We're recent friends."

"I see," he said, mulling that over.

But then his manner softened, possibly in response to Ralph's rendition of "Moonlight in Vermont."

"Dickie and I go back a long way," he said, as if he were doing a voice-over for the nostalgic melody "I used to ride him around in my squad . . . take him to P.J.'s, the Embers, the Stork, give the tootsies at the Latin Quarter a jiggle, both of us taking on a load—and then I'd pour him into the townhouse before the sun came up. I bodyguarded Dickie after I retired and then his wife died—the poet. He took it hard. I thought he'd never get over it—and then he had to go and meet the broad."

"Ilyana," I said, indicating that I had some knowledge of Dickie's history.

"Can you believe it! Went all the way to Hungary to dig up that slut. A fuckin' manicurist in an all-night nail clinic in Budapest. When he could have had the pick of the litter. And now she acts like the Queen Mother. Just look at the way she treats him. She's *starving* the poor bastard."

I glanced across the room in time to see Ilyana snatch a sandwich out of Dickie's hands, then wag her finger at him as if to say, "You naughty boy," before placing the sandwich back on the buffet table.

"This is incredible," he said, pounding on the bar and throwing up his hands. "She wants to get him skinny! And let's say he loses a few pounds. What's he gonna do, jump out of the chair and do a foxtrot? The guy's liable to croak any day now."

"He doesn't look that great."

"He certainly doesn't. And I for one can't take it anymore.

"Wait here," he said, "I'll be right back."

Hands clasped behind his back, whistling innocently like a cartoon cop on his beat, he strolled across the room toward the buffet table.

After waiting for Ilyana to turn to her guests, he picked up half of what looked like a fat corned beef sandwich and slapped it into Dickie Moué's mouth. Then he turned around, shielding Dickie with his big back, and began to bounce innocently on his toes. Raising a shaky hand to steady the half of a sandwich, Dickie took a huge bite out of it, chewed a couple of times and swallowed. At that point, he hesitated, cocking his head as if he had heard his name being paged. He swallowed again, and then his eyes almost came out of his head as he pitched forward and fell on the floor, the sandwich bite still stuck in his throat.

Instinctively, I started across the room to help him, but by the time I reached the buffet table, Irv Gallagher was on his knees trying to get the taste treat out of his mouth. He succeeded, but not entirely; as the crowd gathered, he pounded on Dickie's back, and then began to administer the celebrated Heimlich maneuver, an awkward procedure to pull off with Dickie stretched out on the floor.

When Ilyana saw what had happened, she screamed and said: "I *warned* him about the corned beef."

Then she joined the other guests in looking on anxiously as Gallagher continued trying to revive his old pub-crawling friend, who was not moving.

The first to break away from the crowd was the little old lady I'd hoisted out of the elevator.

"It's too late," she said, gathering a shawl around her. "I saw his color."

She crossed herself solemnly, then broke into a bright smile.

"No point in being gloomy. That won't bring him back. What about joining me for a drink in my room?"

"Not just now," I said, amazed at her boldness.

"I'll be in Penthouse B, in case you change your mind. And don't be frightened. I'm not going to jump on your bones. Unless, of course, you absolutely insist."

Then she sashayed off, leaving me to wonder if there was any limit to her shameful, or shall I say, shameless flirtatiousness. Still, I had to applaud her for feeling and acting like some kind of irresistible temptress, which had the effect of almost turning her into one, though not quite. I marveled at how much more appealing she was than most of the younger women I'd run across, even if, given the choice (and to my everlasting shame) I probably would have picked one of the younger ones. (And that is definitely something we have to correct in America. How long can we continue to ignore the needs of our hot little biddies!)

A team of paramedics arrived soon after and began to work on Dickie, but with no apparent result. They had a whispered conversation, consoled Ilyana and then lifted Dickie on to a stretcher.

"I'd go along," said Ilyana to one of them, "but it wouldn't do any good, right?"

"I doubt it," he said.

And then they carted Dickie out of the hotel.

Frankly, I did not know how to feel. On the one hand, there had been a loss of life, which is never pleasant. And I marveled at the irony of Dickie meeting his end as the result of a delicious corned beef sandwich getting stuck in his throat— the very treat he had coveted and that had been denied to him. I believe one of our novelists has observed that you have to be careful what you wish for—or you may get it. No doubt this is an ancient wisdom, but I feel he should be given credit for shaping it up to fit our own troubled times.

And I had other feelings as well—chief among them relief that my goal had been accomplished despite my not having lifted a finger to help things along.

I returned to the bar in time to hear Ralph announce that he was going to play a medley of Dickie's favorite songs. He began with "Tea for Two," putting a great deal of feeling into it, despite its being on the peppy side.

I was soon joined by Gallagher who mopped at his forehead with a handkerchief and ordered a double bourbon.

"Jesus," he said. "I never saw anything like that in my life. And I'll probably get called up on charges, too. But you saw what happened, Matthew. I was only trying to help out."

"It looked that way to me."

"Thank you. But just you watch! The broad will get everything and Dickie's true friends won't see a dime."

"That's life," I said, a comment I'd found that fit almost any situation.

"It certainly is," said Gallagher.

"Well, my friend," he said, after downing his drink. "I'd better take my leave now and make a voluntary appearance at the station.

"Not to worry," he added with a wink. "I know the guys."

"And here's my card," he said, reaching into his wallet and handing me one. "In case you get caught being naughty."

"Thanks, Irv," I said, glancing at the card, which said:

IRVING GALLAGHER ASSOCIATES
Personal Protection and Industrial Security

"*Zei gesint,* fella," he said. "And don't take any wooden *kreplach.*"

"Zei gesint," I repeated, taking pleasure in learning an exotic new toast.

MY SPIRITS LIFTED considerably as I left the Bancroft and returned to my condo. A case could be made, all things considered, that Dickie was better off where he was—and who was I not to make it.

With some excitement, I called Peabody in Karachi and was somewhat disappointed to learn that he'd already gotten the news.

"You *know* about it?" I said, agog, if that was the correct term, at the speed at which information was passed along to him.

"Oh, yes," he said wearily. "I was informed shortly after it happened."

I picked up a somber note in his voice that troubled me.

"You don't seem too happy about it."

"No, no, I'm delighted. But I've had a bit of a personal setback. Millie was wonderful as Nathan Detroit, incidentally. But after the matinee, I took my wife on a canoeing trip along the Muari River, and it doesn't appear we'll be getting back together."

"I'm sorry to hear that."

"So am I. We fucked, of course, but she's recently buried an aunt and feels that among my five hundred other liabilities that I don't know enough about death."

"I could straighten her out on that."

"What do you mean?" he snapped.

But then he drew back and said: "Oh, *I* see. You're having me on. Do forgive me—I'm not terribly good at satire. But you mustn't let me spoil your good mood. You've accomplished something very special—perhaps not in the expected manner—but it's a success nonetheless, and it's going to put you in an excellent position for the future. I suppose we should celebrate, don't you feel?''

"Why not."

"Well, good. Let me have a look at my calendar. How does your schedule look for the eighteenth?''

"One day is the same as another for me.''

"Let's make it Otis. Ed will no doubt shit when he hears that we've tried another place, but he'll get over it. And I've heard magnificent things about Otis's barbecue. Hot, hot, hot, which is an excellent substitute for all the drinking I've been doing.

"And one more thing, Binny . . .''

"Yes."

"I'm enormously proud of you.''

Chapter Eight

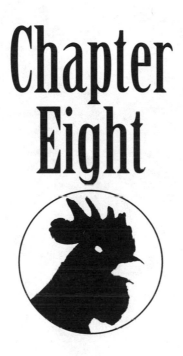

I CALLED LETTIE and told her my job had turned out nicely and that I would be home the following day. Though she could be as lively as a firecracker when she was there in front of you, her phone style was generally detached, bordering on sad. But she was a little more animated than usual on this occasion. She said she had given up her pursuit of an acting career and decided to become a movie producer.

"Will you help me?" she asked. "My friends are not being very supportive."

"I'll do what I can, although I'm not sure I know how to help someone become one."

"Just knowing you're behind me is enough."

After I hung up, I walked over to the shopping area and found a jewelry store that was still open and bought Lettie a diamond choker. I had always wanted to get one for Glo to see it on her pretty neck, but I had never come close to having the funds. And besides, she was dead. So I thought I'd buy one for Lettie that she could hold on to until she got to the age when she was required to attend functions.

I also picked up some young-girl things, such as sweaters and dresses—to balance things out. Each time I bought something for Lettie I felt it was some kind of victory.

LATER IN THE evening, I called the bald girl, which I always knew I would. Though strictly speaking, I had not exactly put in a good day's work, I felt the need to reward myself with a little socializing.

I asked her if she was free to have a drink and, as luck would have it, she said she was.

We met on the patio of a restaurant on Ocean Avenue. I had to fight my way through an army of people to get to it.

Everyone in the world seemed to be in Miami Beach, yet from what I could see, the only thing they did when they got there was form crowds and try to spot Bianca Jagger or someone like that. But I guess that every publication they picked up had told them it was the place to be and to get down there as fast as possible.

The restaurant at which we met was almost deserted, even though it seemed identical to the crowded ones I'd passed along the way. Either there was something wrong with it, or the restaurants got popular street by street, and they hadn't reached our place quite yet.

She had changed her outfit and wore a lacy white blouse and some bluejeans that did not show the outlines of her vagina. She was still bald, of course, but her face seemed softer, to the extent that this is possible in the case of a bald individual. She flickered back and forth between being pretty and quite beautiful. For a split second, she looked like a bald Marilyn Monroe.

I felt a little uneasy about sitting out there in the open with a bald date, but several other hairless girls strolled by, which helped me to relax. So being a little bald was obviously nothing to fall down the steps about in Miami Beach.

"I had an awful fight with Mahmoud," she said. "I finally told him to fuck off and go back to the desert."

"I thought he lived in Chicago."

"He summers there. But his heart is in Riyadh."

"Did he spit on you?"

"Actually not, but in many ways it was worse. At least then, we had some interaction. He said I was untidy."

"How untidy are you?"

"Oh . . . a few leftover eggrolls under the bed . . . some sandwich wrappers here and there . . . but certainly nothing to bust my hump about."

"Then maybe it's for the best," I said, aware that to a degree my comment was self-serving.

She was something of an expert on wines and took a long time studying the list before asking for one that they were out of. So she chose her second favorite. Then we ordered some pasta, which I thought was fine but she felt needed to be ten times spicier.

"He'll never change," she said as she poured on the ground pepper. "His ambition is to live at the Playboy mansion."

"Would Hugh Hefner allow that?"

"Hef?" she said, with a laugh. "Don't be ridiculous."

She twirled some pasta around her fork and then looked up in alarm.

"Oh shit, that's him. Let's get out of here."

I glanced over at the indoor part of the restaurant and indeed saw a sad-looking bearded fellow slumped over the bar, sipping a frosted drink. That was enough for me. The last thing I needed was a knife fight in Miami Beach with a pissed-off Arab.

I threw down some money and followed her across Ocean Road to a dark section of the beach.

"He won't come after us, will he?"

"I doubt it," she said. "He hates sand."

"An *Arab* hates sand?"

"He's definitely in the minority."

"And besides," she added, "*I* crack the whip."

I took a careful look around anyway and when it seemed that the coast was clear, I took her hand, which was attractively clammy, and we strolled along the beach.

"How was your cocktail party?" she asked.

"It was fine until somebody choked to death on a corned beef sandwich."

"The food is awful here," she said.

I was dying to tell her what I was doing at the cocktail party, but it would only have been in the interest of showing off; amazingly, I kept quiet about it. And I'd had it in mind to kiss her, so I thought I might as well do it and get it over with. When I did, she didn't pull away and she didn't get into it either. I could tell she was a veteran of a thousand sudden kisses.

"Feel better now?" she asked.

"A lot."

And I did, having gotten that out of the way. If all else failed, I'd kissed my first bald girl.

We continued our walk along the sand, and she said: "So you're quite the ladies' man, are you."

"What makes you think that?"

She stopped walking, put her hands on her hips like some kind of defiant Southern belle and looked at me squarely.

"Well just how many women *have* you slept with?"

"I don't keep count," I said, which wasn't quite true. "Eight."

She sighed and said: "If you only knew how many men *I've* slept with . . . and the things I had to do with them . . ."

Ordinarily, I get unsettled when I hear about a woman's vast sexual experience—as a younger man I would vomit—but maybe I had changed, since I found myself adopting a roguish and worldly stance.

"Trying to turn me on?" I asked.

"I haven't slept with anyone since I began dating Mahmoud," she said, which I felt was an off-kilter response to my question. "There was my accountant," she continued reflectively. "I owed him a blowjob . . . but I'm not going to start counting that."

Up until that point, I have to admit I wasn't exactly consumed with passion. But there is something about hearing an attractive woman, bald or not, *say* "blowjob"—and I don't even have to get one—that turns me into a different person. Suddenly I was a little bit consumed with passion and pulled her down on the sand where I gave her head a few licks—to get the ball rolling.

"I knew you'd do that." she said.

120

"Was it inappropriate?"

"Only time will tell," she said.

"You'll have to forgive me. I haven't dated for a while—for personal reasons—and I'm a little out of shape in the romance department."

"I find that charming. But this is romance?" she asked in what seemed to be a serious inquiry.

I had a hard time answering that question, and so I didn't. Instead, I held her surprisingly full breasts (why are they always *surprisingly* full?) and kissed her and she said: "You're concentrating on my tits. Try to relax and smell the roses."

That was another one. A woman saying "tits." Next thing I knew she'd say "pussy" and I would become a madman. (And I'm not one of those phone-sex people either. I have to have the individual right there in front of me where I can grab on to her.) And she was right, of course. But how was I not supposed to concentrate on her breasts, or tits, as she preferred. But I tried to put them out of my mind and we rolled around on the sand for a while, where I noted, not with displeasure, that she had elected to go bald throughout. (Normally, when I hit pubic hair, I take it as an indication that I'm home free; but obviously there were to be no such guidelines in this case.) She made some additional corrections in my style, as if I had enrolled in a driver's-ed course. And I had to wonder what it is in my technique that causes women to shout instructions at me while I'm trying to concentrate on making love to them. On the other hand, it was better than that time in America when everybody clammed up in bed, leading to failed marriages and broken hearts.

Carefully following her instructions ("Easy there, fella . . . slow down . . . there you go . . .") I proceeded, in Little Irwin's words, to "do the deed." And I was just about to hit my stride when Mahmoud came out of the shadows, hollering out what I took to be some kind of Arabic imprecation.

121

"Oh, Christ, Mahmoud," she said, sitting up in irritation. "You're doing it *again*."

He lunged at me, and I hit him in the stomach, more out of fear than combat alertness, noting that it was the first punch I'd thrown since lashing out at a rich boy in Tennessee for having too many toys. I waited for a knife to come out, but Mahmoud sat down softly and seemed to be more concerned about the sand in his suit than the tableau he had just witnessed.

"You don't really want her," he said bitterly. "You'll just use her and cast her aside.

"Like stinking fish," he added, invoking (unnecessarily, I felt) some kind of Levantine metaphor.

"How can you be sure of that?" I asked, ignoring the possible truth to his allegation. "Besides, *you're* the one who spits at her."

"How does he know that?" he said, turning to the bald girl, whose name was Laramie, incidentally.

"Oh, stop it, Mahmoud," she said dismissively. "It's practically been written up in the columns."

"Admit it," he said to me. "She's just one of your playthings."

"I'm not Hugh Hefner," I said.

"He knows about Hef, *too*?" he said, glaring at her.

"Right, Mahmoud," she said derisively. "I really had time to recite the whole megillah."

"Don't say megillah," he said.

Then he turned to me and raised his bearded jaw.

"Go ahead. Hit me. See how far it gets you."

It was a strange invitation, considering the circumstances, but before I could respond, the bald girl got to her feet and said: "That's it. I'm through dicking around. Shoo! Both of you. I just want to air out my snatch and get the sand out of my ass."

"Jesus," I said to myself. "This is some person!"

122

Normally, that kind of hot talk from a woman, bald or not, would have sent me halfway to Jupiter and back. But with Mahmoud standing by, I thought it best to keep myself in tow.

"Let's go, Mahmoud," I said. "She's got a point."

We both turned and walked toward the boardwalk, as if we were partners, which in some kind of drawing-room comedy sense, we were.

"And leave the keys under the mat," she called after him.

"Have I ever forgotten?" he shouted back.

"You see what I have to put up with?" he said to me.

"Must be a bitch," I said.

Then, in an attempt to lighten the atmosphere, I asked him what kind of work he did in Miami.

"I'm in a band," he said. "We're trying to get a recording contract. If you know a good agent, I'd appreciate your mentioning my name. I play acoustic guitar."

"I don't happen to know any agents, but what do you do, Arab stuff?"

"Sometimes. It depends on the crowd."

"There must be a lot of competition."

"Tell me about it," he said, then added with blazing eyes. "But we're *very* good."

I could see that it was one thing to roll around on the sand with his girlfriend and quite another to be casual about his music. I thought of asking him to have a drink, maybe finishing off the bottle of wine on the patio, but I felt it might lead to some kind of complex love triangle, and I did not feel that I was up to one. When we reached Ocean Avenue, I slapped him on the shoulder in a show of good fellowship.

"Good luck, Mahmoud."

"The same to you, fella."

Then he reached into his pocket and handed me a card.

"Take this," he said. "We also play at parties and benefits. If things are slow, we'll do a bar mitzvah."

123

* * *

IT WAS UNLIKELY I would see Laramie again. If I got back down to Miami Beach, I might give her a call—not to start up an affair or anything—if something happened, it happened—but just to see how she was doing. And maybe get some more of that hot talk. But I certainly did wish her well. With no hair, a shaky modeling career and a disgruntled Arab boyfriend, she had her hands full.

There are those who would consider the episode a disaster, but I did not see it that way. I had not dated a woman since my tragic loss and was not sure how I would do. Under the circumstances—the bald head, Mahmoud jumping out of the shadows that way—I felt I had performed decently. And though I had not experienced a full-blown romance, I felt I had something to build on.

MY SPIRITS WERE high as I hit the highway the next morning. But as I made my way through the Everglades (taking a shortcut), it occurred to me that the $75,000 I had been advanced might not be mine. And I had already spent a nice chunk of it. It's true that Dickie Moué was out of the picture. But strictly speaking, I had not brought it about. If Peabody's operation wanted to split hairs, they could make the case that I might as well have stayed home. And he would have choked on the corned beef sandwich anyway.

If they wanted to get tough about it, they could claim that I owed them the full $75,000, including the $18,000 that I had spent.

Which, unfortunately, is exactly the position that they took.

Chapter Nine

W E ARE NOT an affluent community, but we are rich in barbecue restaurants and probably have more than we need. Every time you turn around, someone is opening another one, not stopping to think that there are only so many lovers of barbecue to go around.

I had heard of Otis and was aware that it was high up there in the rankings for the excellence of its cuisine. A noted travel guide had awarded it two stars—and would have added a third had they not fallen down on the corn bread. Yet I had never eaten at the restaurant, having been advised that it is best to have a black individual accompany you there. (It is in a poor all-black section of town, which is unfortunately a haven for crime.) It's a sadness of mine that I do not have any black friends—yet at the same time I had never felt it was necessary to just go out there and round some up—just to have some.

If a black person came into my life in the normal course of things, I would welcome him with open arms.

Otis turned out to be a ramshackle place with about a dozen tables, more like somebody's kitchen than a restaurant—and it smelled great. Peabody had gotten there before me and was talking to someone at an adjoining table, a black fellow who had on horn-rimmed glasses and was wearing a business suit and a tie. The fellow had shown him pictures of his two children, and Peabody was carrying on about them as though he had never seen pictures of kids before.

"Come over here, Binny," he said. "You've got to see these pictures. They're remarkable. And this is Leonard—he's a management consultant. Extraordinary fellow."

I said hello to Leonard and looked at the pictures and thought they were nice, although truthfully I didn't see anything remarkable about them. Nor did Leonard come across as

127

being extraordinary. But Peabody thought otherwise. He soon learned that Leonard had a house on the lake and owned a sailboat, which Peabody thought was remarkable, too. He obviously felt that the way to deal with black people was to make a huge fuss over them—and you would get credit for being a liberal-minded fellow. I do not make a fuss over black people unless there is something to make a fuss about—which to my mind makes me an *authentically* liberal-minded person.

But try explaining that to Peabody.

He and the black executive exchanged phone numbers, and he finally turned to me.

"Fascinating fellow, isn't he? But where's Lettie? I thought surely you'd bring her along."

I said she had her schoolwork to do, although I knew she was back at the house and probably parading around in her choker. I wasn't sure how she would feel about it, but she had loved it and wanted to wear it to school. Though I did not think it was appropriate for a schoolgirl to come to class in a diamond choker, I compromised and said she could wear it to school and show it to her girlfriends while I waited in the schoolyard. And then I would take it back to the house with me, which I did.

"I'm *so* disappointed," he said. "She's lovely, and I feel certain she'd like me. Besides, I think it's important that a young girl at some point be exposed to an older and somewhat sophisticated man."

I wondered how he knew that Lettie was lovely and once again concluded that it was probably Ed Bivens who had given him a report on her looks. As to the need for her to be exposed to an older, sophisticated man, I wasn't too sure about that. No doubt she would come in contact with one in due time. Which is not to say that it could really hurt for her to meet Peabody. If nothing else, she would probably enjoy his English accent, which I certainly did.

"Why not come over to the house for a drink sometime," I suggested.

"Unless you have cats."

"Are you allergic to them?"

"I don't like animals," he said, pursing his lips, which for a second made him *look* like an animal.

"We do have a few cats."

"I was afraid of that. But thank you for the invitation all the same."

We ordered buckets of ribs and diet cokes, which is the only drink they serve. Peabody picked up a rib, inspected it, discarded it, then picked up another and discarded that one, too. He looked over some others, put them back and finally shoved the bowl aside.

"They're not very good, are they."

I hadn't tried one yet, but considering all the awards that Otis had won, I could not imagine that they would be anything but superior. But before I could sample one for myself, Peabody had called over the waitress and ordered cheeseburgers for us as a substitute.

Then he leaned across the table, his eyes moist with emotion.

"We did it, didn't we, Binny . . ."

"We certainly did," I said, letting the "we" part slide by.

We reminisced about our modest start at the Ed Bivens Diner and how beautifully it had all come together in Miami Beach.

"He was a prick, wasn't he?"

"Who's that?" I asked.

"Dickie."

"I didn't really get to know him."

"You wouldn't have cared for him, trust me."

We ate our cheeseburgers, which were decent enough, although frankly, they put me in the mood for ribs. After a decent interval, and half knowing what his response would be, I brought up the subject of money.

"Oh, my God," he said in alarm, pushing back from the table. "You haven't *spent* any of it, have you?"

"Actually, I did. Around $18,000."

"I wish you hadn't done that, Binny. After all, it's not as if it was yours. You really didn't *do* anything."

"There wasn't anything to do."

"Yes, I suppose you could look at it that way. And I'm not minimizing your contribution, but it's not as if you were hands on.

"Dear me," he said, looking around, as if for help. "We do have a situation, don't we? But you mustn't be upset about it. I always work with people at least twice, and we can apply the money you've gone through to a new venture. And we'll raise the fee for this next go-round to $250,000. How does that sound?"

I said it sounded good, which, of course, it did.

"Excellent. There's just one other chap I work with in Rawalpindi who has some ability. But I've lost a bit of confidence in him, quite frankly. And my feeling is that you really should continue in this, Binny. You're *very* good."

I thanked him and decided that as long as we were on a roll, I would tell him about my idea for removing northern fowl mites from caged layer hens. I had always thought it was a surefire business opportunity, but I could never find anyone willing to invest in it.

"I believe in it with all my heart, Valentine," I said, after I had described it in detail. "Even though it's been a family joke for years. My poor wife would always say: 'There goes Binns again with his crazy northern fowl mite scheme.' I'd stop people on the street and tell them about it."

"I'm sure you did," said Peabody. "Now look here, don't take this personally, but I'm afraid I wouldn't be any good at it. I just don't have a feel for that sort of thing. It's quite sound, I'm sure, and I suppose if it were further along, I might consider coming in on it. But I just *know* when things aren't right for me. I'm sure you understand."

I told him I understood entirely, but in truth I was tremendously upset. For one thing, his cool response had the effect of making me lose confidence in an idea that I had always believed in and felt would be of great interest to anyone in poultry. Then, too, I felt he had let me down. I had gone along with *his* scheme, and we had had a success together. (He was welcome to put an astcrisk next to the "success" part, if he so chose.)

But now *I* had a proposal and he had turned me down flat.

I pretended to be cheerful as we finished up our dinner, but in truth I was angry if not enraged. And I knew it was the type of injury that I would carry around for years.

We made a date to meet at his office the following day, which I agreed to halfheartedly, feeling that I was being yanked around like a puppet. What I really wanted to do was take my idea to someone else—maybe Ted Feather up in Winnipeg— have it turn out to be a tremendous success and then quietly lord it over Peabody.

I RETURNED HOME and found Lettie asleep in her bed, and still wearing the choker. Rather than take the chance of waking her, I decided to let hcr go ahead and sleep with the choker around her neck. Pretending I was a wizard, I made a whistling sound— and blew some imaginary sleep dust in her eyes—as was my custom each night when I tucked her in.

Then I went into the bathroom to wash up, and as I toweled myself down, I spotted an open box of tampons on the shelf—with two of them missing. The school nurse had warned me that something like that would happen, but I was a little thrown nonetheless. The new development must have come about while I was in Miami Beach, dealing with the Dickie Moué project, and I only hoped that the nurse and Lettie's girlfriends had combined to see her through. She kept a copy of a book

called, *What Every Girl Should Know* on her nightstand, and I
imagined there was a helpful chapter in there as well.

Even if I had been there, I'm not sure what I could have
done to help. Though I have enormous respect for women and
applaud their recent and long overdue gains, I do not know that
much about their internal workings. I had promised myself to
brush up on the subject, but I had never gotten around to it.
Having spent most of my life in poultry, I knew there were eggs
involved, but as to ovaries and fallopian tubes and that type of
thing, it is all a mystery to me. I *still* wasn't sure what I could do
for her other than to accept what had transpired manfully, give
her extra hugs—as if such a thing was possible—and hope for
the best.

I checked to make sure the rest of the money was still inside my Capons team jacket. It was, and though strictly speaking, it wasn't quite mine—indeed one might argue that I was
$18,000 in the hole—at least Lettie and I had some financial
security for the difficult days ahead.

This in turn may have caused my anger at Peabody to sub-
side. Maybe it had been too much to ask him to appreciate my
northern fowl mite procedure. Though it was hard for me to
admit it, I was aware of a flaw in the second stage of the applica-
tion, and it was possible that Peabody, with that sixth sense of
his, had smoked it out.

That would mean that I had gotten angry at him for my
own deficiencies.

Once that became clear, I decided to get rid of any rancor-
ous feelings I had toward the man and to show up for our meeting with a positive attitude and an open heart.

WE GOT HIT with an angry rain the next morning. There are
those who would take that as a bad omen, but I am not among
them. All it meant to me is that I would have trouble getting
Lettie to wear her yellow raincoat.

"It makes me look fat," she said. "And my generation doesn't wear raincoats."

"Well, my generation does," I said. "So keep it on."

It was amazing. She and Glo had gone after each other like cats and dogs. Yet Lettie and I had never had a cross word between us. Perhaps it was because I was the only game in town. Or maybe we just loved each other to distraction.

As I drove her to school in the Trooper, I checked to see if there was any difference in her because of the tampons, but all I could detect was that she had become mushier and kept her head against my shoulder for the whole ride.

I was soaked to the bone when I arrived at Peabody's office, which would not have bothered me if it hadn't been for my wet feet. I told Peabody that I could not concentrate when I was in that state, and I asked if he'd mind my running over to the K-Mart to pick up a six-pack of dry socks.

"That's out of the question," he said curtly.

"But I can't be at my best with wet feet."

"I'm afraid you don't understand," he said, taking me by the shoulders as if I was a disobedient child. "There's a call coming through momentarily, and it's tremendously important that you be here. If we lose this fellow, I'm not sure how we'd be able to proceed. Probably put off the operation until next season when God knows what we'll all be doing."

Despite his explanation, I was tempted to run over to the K-Mart anyway. I *really* do have trouble with wet feet, and I'm sure I'm not the only one. I cited the example of Napoleon's troops getting bogged down in Russia because of the same problem, but I might as well have been talking in a foreign language. He simply shook his head in silent exasperation and would not budge.

As a compromise, I got some Scott towels from the bathroom and dried my feet in front of him, making sure to get between the toes. He looked away as I did so, and I'm not sure I

133

wouldn't have done the same had he dried his feet flamboyantly in *my* presence.

When the call came through, my feet were freezing, and I was *still* uncomfortable, but at least they were dry.

"Kevin Kurosawa here," said the voice on the phone. "How are you guys doing?"

"We're fine," said Peabody. "I have Binny with me, and I thought you two should have a chat before we get under way."

"That's fine with me," said Kevin. "It's a pleasure to meet you, Binns. Val told me quite a bit about you and I understand you're quite a guy."

"I hear you're quite a guy, too," I said, taking some liberty here since Peabody hadn't told me what kind of guy he was.

"Thanks," he said, clearing his throat. "So you're in the chicken business. Well, my wife and I eat a lot of chicken, and we can't say enough about it. And by the way, what do you think of those Lakers!"

The question caught me off guard since actually I had not given any thought to the Lakers. Though I was familiar with the name and knew they were a basketball franchise, I did not take any particular interest in the sport and allowed as much on the phone.

"I don't follow them," I said.

"Oh," said Kevin, who appeared to lose interest in the conversation.

I thought I had blown the deal, but to his credit, Peabody did not throw up his hands in frustration.

To the contrary, he looked on with amusement.

I made an attempt to recover by telling Kevin about Lettie's great interest in basketball.

"I haven't gotten around to it, but I plan to attach a hoop to the back of the cottage so she can see if she's any good at it."

That seemed to perk him up a bit and he recited some statistics on the growth of women's collegiate basketball around the country.

"Women will never make it in the NBA, Binns. I have to be honest. They're dead in big-time basketball. They *are* good though, I'll give them that, and they *enjoy* the game, which in the final analysis is what really counts."

"That's all we can expect of them."

"Exactly my sentiments. I could not have put it more succinctly. Have I used that word correctly?"

"I believe so."

"Thank you, Binns. And I can see that you're my kind of guy. If it's all right with you, I'm ready to go at my end."

"Binny and I are ready to go at ours," said Peabody.

"Then we're all set. And put up that hoop, Binns. Your daughter will like it. She'll never make it in the NBA, and it's going to hurt. It's going to hurt real bad. You might as well get used to that. But she'll benefit healthwise and you will not regret it.

"I'll get on it as soon as I get back to the cottage."

And that's the note on which we concluded our conversation.

"How do you feel it went?" Peabody asked.

I said I thought it went well, which I did, apart from my minor gaffe about the Lakers and considering it was my first conference call.

"And what did you think of Kevin?"

"He seemed like a decent enough fellow."

"I'm not so sure of him myself. He's working for us on a temporary basis, and we're trying to get him something over at CBS as a sportscaster, which is his true love. Did you feel any chemistry?"

"Not particularly," I said. "But I didn't feel any lack of it either."

"Now look, Binny," he said, taking me by the shoulders again and fixing me with his clear blue eyes. "It's terribly important that you get along, since you and Kevin are going to be working closely. If you have any reservations, tell me what they are, although frankly I don't know who else we can find at this late date.''

"We'll get along fine.''

"I hope so,'' he said without confidence.

He told me that the targeted individual was a Japanese industrialist named Matsumoto who lived in Tokyo and who had frustrated Thomas Gnu on a business deal at a delicate stage of his career.

"Gnu had vowed that he would have his first billion by the time he reached the age of forty. He and Matsumoto were part owners of a tool-and-die company in Peshawar. While Gnu was away at a tennis tournament, Matsumoto conspired with the other directors to have Gnu lose his seat on the board. As a result, Gnu fell short of his goal and had to wait two years before he reached it.''

"But he *did* get his billion,'' I put in.

"When he was forty-two.''

"And that's been eating away at him?''

"You don't know Gnu. Have you been to Tokyo?''

"No, but I've heard a lot about it.''

"I think you'll like it. What I thought I'd do is pop over and see you, once you've finished up your business—and we would tool around the Ginza together, have a bit of fun.''

I said that ordinarily I'd enjoy that, but it was important that I get back as soon as possible so I could be with Lettie—although I didn't say why.

"Probably got her period, eh?''

"How'd you know that?'' I said sharply, annoyed by this invasion of our privacy and amazed that he could have gotten this information.

"It's written all over your face.''

"Lettie's period is written all over my *face*?''

"You're such a child sometimes," he said peevishly. "Very well, then, return to your precious daughter."

"I haven't even been to Japan yet."

"Whatever," he said, and began to shuffle some papers.

I was upset with him until I realized that despite his suave exterior and his vast global connections, Peabody was a lonely fellow, and I had hurt his feelings.

"Well, look," I said, "if it's really important to you, I suppose we could hang out for a bit—after I take care of Matsumoto."

"No, no," he said, picking up a little voice recorder. "And if you'll forgive me, I have some reports to get out."

He switched on the recorder and began to dictate in a whisper.

"It is the military-industrial complex that continues to influence the world markets. The Christian Coalition as well should be taken into consideration . . ."

I could see that he was involved in global affairs, and there was little for me to do at this point.

And so we parted on a cool note.

Chapter
Ten

MY ITINERARY AND travel documents arrived as per schedule the next morning. Tucked into my passport was a form note that said I'd be expected to pay my own expenses—due to the substantial fees that I was to receive and the sky-rocketing cost of living in Japan. That threw me off momentarily. There was plenty of money left from the advances, but if I paid my own way, I'd be deeper in the hole—at least until I got the job done. This new development made me all the more determined to bring it off successfully; I only hoped that because of my West ern features, I did not stand out too prominently in the country of Japan.

Lettie took the news of my trip calmly and asked if I could pick up an agent for her while I was over there, for her acting and producing. I said I'd see if I could find one, although I couldn't figure out why she'd want a Japanese agent when there were so many American ones to choose from.

"Trust me," she said. "It's a good career move."

I called Edwina's mother and asked if Lettie and the cats could stay with her while I was away, and she said it was the least she could offer after all I had done for her daughter. I couldn't think of exactly what I had done for Edwina, unless it was the compliment I had paid her on the new glasses she had to wear.

"Contrary to current thought," I had told her, "men do make passes at girls who wear glasses."

My comment caused her to giggle and come out of her slouch.

So maybe that was it.

Before I left, I stopped at the new mall and bought Peabody an expensive leather credit card holder, which I had sent over to his office in the hope that it would smooth over our mild contretemps.

After driving over to Dallas, I parked the Trooper at the airport and, as instructed, purchased a round-trip first-class ticket to Tokyo. An economy-class ticket would have been fine with me, but that's not what they wanted, no doubt because of their corporate image.

The price of the ticket astonished me. If it was any indication of how much things cost in Japan, I could see I would be broke by the time I got back.

The trip went smoothly enough and you would think I was royalty the way the attendants fussed over me. I peeked back at the economy section and saw that they were fussing over those passengers, too, although not half as much as they were fussing over me.

After we landed, I lined up at Customs and Immigration and got a little nervous over the way they treated the fellow in front of me. He was an older gentleman with close-cropped silver hair who carried a briefcase and was dressed in an elegant tweed suit. In sum, he was the picture of professorial elegance. Yet they could not have been more disrespectful to him. They poked at his chest, shouted in his face and finally carted him off somewhere, no doubt for some serious questioning. I thought to myself that if they could treat a distinguished-looking fellow like that so shabbily, I could just about imagine how they would deal with me. Yet to my surprise, they just waved me through with barely a glance at my documents.

Though, obviously, I was far from innocent in my intentions, something in my demeanor must have given off an impression of respectability.

So maybe I was cut out for this kind of work after all.

I was aware that the Japanese have been criticized for harsh trading practices and for occasionally striking out at their neighbors. But on a personal level, I found the average individual to be unfailingly courteous and polite. While I was waiting for the bus, I pulled out a slim cigar for the purpose of relaxation; no sooner had I brought it to my lips than several fellows came dashing forward to offer me a light, one of them insisting that I keep his lighter (which was not, incidentally, of the cheap throwaway variety). I protested, but finally put it in my pocket, taking note of his exceptional kindness.

Soon afterward, a little old lady with a knapsack on her back, asked me if she could practice her English on me, which I agreed to let her do. She was all over the map on her pronunciation and sentence structure, but who could fail to give her credit for taking on a new language at her advanced age.

How many Americans would do the same?

From the accounts I had read, I pictured the Japanese as being all bunched together, practically lying on top of one another. Yet judging from what I saw from the bus window, they had space to spare. There were fields and meadows along the highway, and you could have relocated a ton of them right there. There were also picturesque little farms and tiny factories, and here and there a giant red horse stuck out in the fields, all by itself, perhaps as a proud reminder of their imperial splendor in times gone by.

Looking at those proud yet playful red horses, I felt as if I had stepped into a fairytale.

My hotel had a giant lobby. Here again, I wondered how the Japanese people could complain about their lack of space and then go ahead and have a lobby that was as big as a small town. My feelings were confirmed when I saw my tiny room—not that there wasn't everything I needed in there once I had stopped being offended and looked around.

As an example, there were twenty different kinds of teas lined up on a vanity table. (I am not a tea drinker, but that is beside the point.) Yet for all the conveniences, I could barely stand up in the little room, which made me wonder, once again, why they hadn't carved up some of the giant lobby and attached it on to the little rooms for added comfort.

It seemed important for them to put on an impressive

front; no doubt this was due to their complex culture and their weird and isolated position on the map.

Since my appointment with Kevin was not until the early evening, I took a little walk around the hotel and soon realized I was in the home district of a mystery writer whose work I admired. His books featured the world's most patient detective, who had solved one murder case by walking for miles along a railroad track, looking for clues that the murderer may have thrown out of a window.

Naturally, he spotted one, due to his patience.

I found a stretch of railroad track, and to amuse myself, I followed it for a while, pretending I was that detective. But I soon ran out of patience and decided to get some lunch.

The first restaurant I came to had a sign above it that said, CHINESE FOOD, and I thought I'd try it, just as a novelty. I had come down with a cold on the way over and decided to get some soup to see if I could clear it up. There was a picture of a soup bowl on the menu, and when the waitress came by, I pointed to it; she got the idea and before long had placed a big bowl in front of me that had everything in it but the kitchen sink. By the time I got halfway through with it, my cold was gone, just as if I'd spent a month in the country.

And I could hardly wait to tell Lettie that I had had the best *Chinese* food I'd ever eaten, in *Japan* of all places.

To put myself over the top, I *did* have a cup of green tea and then I returned to my hotel to prepare for the meeting with Kevin Kurosawa.

Along the way, I spotted exactly one homeless person, a cheery fellow with a red nose and a nice-sized paunch, who was stretched out comfortably on a grass highway divider. Except for a hole in his shoe, he was neatly dressed and seemed to be having the time of his life, waving to passersby, some of whom came over and presented him with bunches of flowers and colorfully wrapped gift packages. Far from bringing down the neighborhood, you could argue that he had spruced it up. I concluded that the Japanese certainly did have a handle on their homeless problem. Shouldn't they be given credit for that? (Unless they had them all stashed away in some section that I had not visited—which I doubt. They don't seem to be that way.)

I HAD SENT my blue suit jacket with the gold buttons down to the valet for a quick dry cleaning, and when I showed up at my room, a delegation of six fellows was there, each one with a long explanation of why they could not get a spot out of the sleeve. It must have been a blow to their national pride, and they apologized profusely. I said I understood, and they said they appreciated that and finally bowed out of my room, leaving me some cookies. Though the cookies were excellent, the visit resulted in my being twenty minutes late for my appointment. It was at a club in the Rappongi area that was not easy to find, which didn't help matters.

As I stepped out of the cab, I saw a tall, wiry fellow pacing up and down in the front of the club and chewing his lip while a plumpish and pleasant-looking American woman looked on patiently. He had on a business suit and tie, with his shirt collar open, and he wore a black patch over one eye. As I approached the club, he appeared to recognize me. Since I did not know another soul in the whole country, I gathered, correctly as it turned out, that this could only be Kevin Kurosawa.

"Jesus Christ, Binns," he said, holding his head in his hands and charging forward to greet me. "What *happened*? I thought you'd never get here. I was worried sick, and it's a good thing my wife was here to calm me down. She's the sane one in the family, and I'm lucky to be married to her. Sandy has stuck with me for twenty years and believe me, I'm not that easy to live with. I'd be *nothing* without her, Binns. *Nothing!*

"Say hello to Sandy."

I shook hands with Kevin's wife and apologized for being

late, telling them about the dry cleaners and how they were unable to get the spot out of my suit jacket.

"That's understandable, Binns," said Kevin. "You're in a foreign country. Try not to forget that. You may not approve of the way they do things, but it *is* their country, and they have a perfect right to do things their way. Would you agree to that?"

"Yes, I would."

"Some of the things they do, such as their worship of *Madonna*—and don't get me wrong, she's got a lot of talent—some of the things they do turn my stomach. But I *am* half Japanese and proud of it. Anybody who insults them, I'll put them right through a wall. Isn't that correct, Sandy?"

"Yes, it is," said his mild-mannered wife.

I told Kevin that I had no intention of saying anything against the Japanese people, which seemed to satisfy him. Then I took a good look at him and saw that he did indeed appear to be half-Japanese. His hair and his one good eye and his nose were all Japanese-looking. The same held true for his sloping belly, which I had noticed on other Japanese fellows. Yet apart from those features, he could have passed for an American.

I followed Kevin and Sandy into the club, a huge, noisy space that was decorated in purple and chrome and that I found to be on the flashy side. Most of the club members were young men in business suits who appeared to be half-Japanese and half-American, just as Kevin was.

Though the club was named the Blue Parrot, I thought a more appropriate name would be the Half and Half, although obviously the owners didn't see it that way.

After we had sat down at one of the chrome tables and ordered drinks, Kevin said: "Admit it, Binns. You want to know about the eye. Don't be embarrassed. I can't say that I blame you. If the situation was reversed, I'd want to hear about *your* eye."

I said I wouldn't mind hearing about the eye, but only if he wanted to tell me about it.

"I appreciate that, Binns. You're a gentleman. Val told me you had excellent manners, and I can see that he was right. Doesn't he have excellent manners, Sandy?"

"Yes, he does," said Sandy, a bit uncomfortably.

"Here's the scoop. My stepfather nicked me with a dart in the rathskeller of our home in suburban Illinois. Some say it was deliberate—the sonofabitch *did* hate me, although I have to admit he treated mom like a queen. But what are you gonna do! It's true I missed out on the state basketball championship and to this day, my fallaway jumper sucks—I *can* still drive to the hoop—but that's life. I had a choice—piss and moan, or get on with my life, which I did, with the assistance of my lovely wife who you just met.

"Without Sandy," he said, pounding the table, "I'd be dogmeat, Binns. *Dogmeat.*"

"I lost *my* wife," I told him, supportively. "And without her *I* would have been dogmeat. For all I know I may *be* dogmeat anyway."

"You're not dogmeat," said Kevin. "If you were, we would have heard about it. Don't be so hard on yourself."

"I'm sorry to hear about your wife," said Sandy, breaking her silence and covering my hand with hers.

"You see that, Binns," said Kevin. "You see how sensitive she is. God knows where I'd be without her. I don't even want to think about it. And *I'm* sorry to hear about your wife, too. Anytime you want to talk about it, any hour of the day or night, I'll be there. Just don't insult my people, that's all I ask."

"I would never do that."

"Good. I knew I could count on you."

One of the half-Japanese and half-American fellows approached us, tapped Kevin on the shoulder and pointed to the rear of the club where a dozen young executive types were seated around a banquet table.

"We're all waiting for you, Kev," he said.

"Tell them not to get nervous. I'll be right over."

Then he turned to me and said: "Forgive me, Binns. I rarely do this, and Sandy will tell you I'm one of the most considerate people you'll ever meet. But I have to give an inspirational speech to those putzes back there. I plan to lead off with a story about a cross-country trip I took with my brother-in-law in the spring of '76. It's a terrific yarn, but there's a possibility that they might not get it. If they don't, all I can say is fuck 'em.

"Sorry, Sandy," he said, catching himself and burying his head in his hands. "Jesus Christ, when will I ever learn not to talk that way in front of her."

"That's all right, Kev," she said.

"Thank you, Sandy," he said. "That's very understanding of you. I'll be right back."

Sandy and I watched him cross the room to the banquet table and begin his speech. The young executives listened intently to him, but after a while they turned to each other with puzzled looks and began to squirm around in their seats, as if they were miserable. Whatever misgivings Kevin had about his opening anecdote were apparently justified.

Since Sandy was not the conversational type, I took a minute to think about her husband. That he was a nonstop talker was evident. If there was something to say, he would say it. But as a listener, you could sit back and coast along on the shoulders, so to speak, of all that conversation, which was relaxing. He also seemed to be a sincere and open-mannered fellow who wore his heart on his sleeve. And I had no doubt that he would show up at any hour of the day or night if you needed him. The question was whether you wanted him to do that. And I had the feeling that he would show up whether you needed him or not. Finally, I was not sure he was the type of fellow you'd want to have along on a sensitive assignment, such as the one I had been given. But he had been chosen as my liaison man, which meant that Peabody must have seen something in him, just as he had spotted something in me.

Some ten minutes later, Kevin returned to our table, sweating and mopping at his forehead with a napkin.

"Can you believe it," he said. "They hated the story. And all I can say is fuck 'em. Excuse me again, Sandy."

"That's perfectly all right, Kev."

"Didn't you sort of know they wouldn't like it?" I said.

"You're right. I cannot *believe* how perceptive you are. I *knew* they would hate it, and I went ahead and told it anyway.

"I must be crazy," he said, smacking his head.

"You're not crazy, Kev," said Sandy.

"Thank you, Sandy. You weren't sitting over here and smirking at me, were you, Binns?"

"No, I wasn't."

"I thought you were. And it threw off my timing."

"I don't think he was, Kev," said Sandy.

"If you say so, Sandy. But it sure looked that way to me."

Rather than continue to insist that I hadn't smirked—which is not in my nature—I decided to push on to more serious matters.

"What about Matsumoto?" I asked, lowering my voice in a professional manner.

"I'm glad you asked that question, Binns. Val said you were a hard-working fellow, and I can see that you are. He also said you were brilliant, *brilliant,* and I can see that, too. Not that it gives you the right to smirk during one of my stories."

"I didn't smirk."

"All right, all right," he said, mopping at his forehead with his sleeve. "Don't get hot. Jesus *Christ* you're sensitive. If you say you didn't smirk, you didn't smirk, and I'm willing to drop it, even though it'll probably bother me for years . . ."

"Tell him about Matsumoto, Kevin," said Sandy.

"What?" he asked, looking puzzled. "Oh, yeah. Now I'm sorry to have to tell you this, Binns, but Matsumoto is a prince among men."

"I'm sorry to hear that."

149

"I knew you would be. His workers worship the ground he walks on. I myself did PR for the man, and I have never been treated more decently. He said I could go back to work for him anytime I wanted to, and I have no reason to doubt his sincerity. You won't meet many people like that, and I may have to take him up on his offer since I'm strapped for money these days. But don't worry, I'm not going to hit you up for a loan, although I'd pay it back at the first opportunity, and there'd be no reason for you to lose any sleep over it."

"I'm in kind of a hole myself these days."

"I respect that, Binns, and I appreciate your honesty, although I wasn't going to ask for much. But we'll let that go."

"He must have *some* faults," I said, changing the subject quickly.

"He does have *one,*" he said, "but I'd rather not tell you about it in front of Sandy. Excuse us, darling."

"You go right ahead and take care of your business, Kev."

"Thanks, Sandy."

"What a doll," he said.

Then he took me aside and shielded his mouth with one hand.

"About the only thing I can come up with is that Matsumoto can't fuck the same woman twice."

"What's that all about?"

"Beats me, Binns. I can't make head or tail out of it."

"Is he married?"

"Divorced. Fucked her once and that was it."

"How do I get a shot at him?" I asked, somewhat metaphorically.

"I'll show you where he lives after dinner. Now let's get back to Sandy. God knows we've kept her waiting long enough."

AFTER WE HAD eaten our sushi dinners, which were excellent, Kevin and Sandy drove me out to Matsumoto's house, which was situated in a quiet working-class neighborhood nearby. In marked contrast to the modest little frame houses that surrounded it, his place looked like a New York City skyscraper that had been shrunk down in size, while retaining its correct proportions. Unless I was mistaken, it was tilted slightly, as if a giant had used it as a plaything, then got tired of it and stuck it in the ground.

There were some security guards at the front of the property who looked around warily as we drove by, and I could see that it was going to be difficult to get at Matsumoto in his place of residence. I pictured him walking around up there or perhaps watching some TV—or doing whatever he was doing at a tilted angle.

"We're out of luck, Binns," said Kevin, taking note of the tight security. "But I did want you to see where the man lives— right in the middle of his workers. He wanted to have a house just like theirs, but his directors were dead set against it. They felt his house should stand out, and I don't blame them.

"The man is a saint, although it kills me to have to tell you that."

"That's fine," I said, "he's a saint. But how do we get at him?"

"Excellent question," said Kevin as we left the neighborhood. "Jesus *Christ* you're on the ball. But I'm way ahead of you. It hurts me to tell you this, but his workers are giving a parade for the man tomorrow, in honor of all the wonderful things he's done for them. I *do* have a few connections left—not everyone has turned their backs on me—and I'll get you into that parade. I'll drive you there tomorrow, even though it's out of my way. And I'll take you back to the hotel now, although *that's* out of my way, too."

"What about a cab?"

"No cab will pick you up at this hour because of your Western features, although I'd appreciate it if you don't hold that against my countrymen. If you do, we may have to duke it out.

You're a little bigger than I am and can probably kick the shit out of me, but you never know. I have fast hands.''

"I won't hold it against them.''

"Thanks, Binns. Where's *your* home incidentally?''

I told him where I lived, and he asked if it happened to be near the ocean.

"No, it's not.''

"What about a lake?''

"No, sir.''

"Not even a river?'' he said.

"We do have a river that cuts through town, although it's mostly for show and doesn't have any commercial traffic on it.''

"Is that right,'' said Kevin. "Well, maybe it will someday, you never know. As a matter of fact, Sandy and I have always wanted to be near a river. We're going to be in your area next month and might drop by for a visit. Not that we'd expect you to put us up, although if the situation was reversed, you could stay with us for as long as you like.''

Seeing that he had boxed me in and that I had no choice, I said that he could stay with me and Lettie.

"That's great,'' said Kevin. "Now Lettie is your daughter, am I right? And I understand she got her period.''

"How did you find that out?'' I said, feeling my blood pressure go up a notch or two.

"Oh, Jesus,'' said Kevin, who couldn't have failed to notice my irritation. "I can see you're touchy about it, and I'm sorry I brought it up. But I would like to add—if you'll bear with me— that it's perfectly natural and nothing to be ashamed of. My sister, God bless her, got *her* period and is now a highly successful office manager in Edgemere, New Jersey. Sandy? The same thing, and I don't have to tell you how *she* turned out. It's part of life, Binns, and you might as well get used to it.''

"I don't need the whole world to know about it. And don't call me Binns.''

"Sorry about that. Do you prefer being called 'Binny'?''

"Try Matthew T. Morning."

"Matthew T. Morning," he repeated softly trying out the name for himself. Seemingly satisfied, he said: "You got it. And you *do* have a point. I swear on my life, and Sandy's life, too, that I'll never say another word about your daughter's period. I made a mistake. I *am* human. And thanks again for the invitation to stay with you and your lovely daughter. Not a word from now on about her period. The invitation is still on, isn't it?"

"Yes, it is."

"Great. And I promise we won't be any trouble."

THEY DROPPED ME off at the hotel, and I made a mental note to tell Peabody—next time I talked to him—that I did not appreciate his broadcasting the news about Lettie's period to the whole world. I felt strongly that my personal affairs should be kept private, especially when they were of such a sensitive nature. That held true no matter how much money I was being paid—not that I had earned any of it so far.

And I was upset about Matsumoto, too. Far from being the despicable individual Peabody had made him out to be, he had turned out to be a decent sort and highly respected, exactly the kind of fellow who might respond to my northern fowl mite procedure, although obviously, it would be awkward presenting it to him under the circumstances.

What had I gotten myself into? First there was Dickie Moué in his wheelchair. Now it was Matsumoto who was revered by his employees. It was true that he could only sleep with the same woman once, but that could have related to some psychological flaw buried deep in his childhood. And it was certainly no justification for taking the man's life, although some feminist groups might disagree.

Yet who among us, I would argue to them, does not have some human frailty?

I thought of calling Peabody and telling him to count me

out, but I knew that this was just bravado on my part. The day I'd signed on with him, I had crossed a line, and there was no turning back. Once embarked on a course of action, I have always found it virtually impossible to switch gears, a trait that Peabody had probably detected in me.

Nonetheless, I was restless. Since sleep was out of the question, I decided to take advantage of the hotel's massage service, which was listed prominently in the guest directory.

In truth, I was hoping for a bright young thing to show up and was somewhat disappointed when a toothless little grandmother appeared at my door. Perhaps I should have been more specific about my requirements.

She turned out to be a tough old bird. She flipped me over on my stomach, jumped up on my back and began to stomp all over me with her rough and ancient feet. Each time I looked around to see what she was up to, she smacked my head and indicated that I was to mind my own business. I thought she would break my back, but she stopped just short of doing that. Despite her rough technique, it turned out that she knew what she was doing. When she finally hopped off my back, I was limp as a dishrag and ready to go to bed.

I consoled myself by thinking that a beautiful young woman would not have done half so good a job.

And when I woke up the next morning, I saw that she had shined my shoes for no extra charge.

Chapter
Eleven

KEVIN SHOWED UP bright and early and immediately apologized for his wife's absence.

"That was a wild night we all had and putting two of them back to back would have been a strain. She also had to rest up for her pearl-diving class. But Sandy thought you were a wonderful guy, and I want to thank you for making me look good."

"Not at all," I said, wondering what was so wild about the previous night, which had seemed uneventful to me. And I did not point out that she seemed a little mature to be getting into pearl diving.

"Sandy also agreed with you that it was wrong of me to bring up your daughter's period—so you can relax on that score."

"Let's get going," I said.

We headed for the outskirts of Tokyo and after three hours of driving, we hit a range of mountains, which surprised me. I knew about Mt. Fuji, of course, but did not realize that Japan had some other less famous mountains as well.

After parking at the foot of one, we made our way to what appeared to be a recreational area. It had a row of little gift shops, and I considered stopping at one and picking up some souvenirs for Lettie, but decided a wise course would be to purchase them on the way home, assuming I made it back safely.

Kevin said the parade was in a picnic area on top of the mountain. Then he led me to the chairlift that took visitors up there. After we had strapped ourselves in and started up the mountain, he casually handed me a gun and a silencer and told me to put both items in my pocket.

"Val told me to give them to you."

It amazed me that he could go on and on about trivial

157

matters yet be so nonchalant when it came to issues of substance.

I did not know the precise designation of the weapon, but it was the heaviest one I had ever handled and felt bulky in my suit jacket. I took it out and slipped it under my belt, along with the silencer, hoping that the gun would not accidentally shoot off my hip.

"You *do* know what you're doing, don't you?" said Kevin.

"Don't worry about a thing," I said with a confidence I did not truthfully feel.

We traveled up along the hills, taking in the scenic wonders below.

"Isn't it great," said Kevin. "And here I was—worried about a pissy little sportscasting job at a major network when I can have this!"

"Who said you can't have both?"

"That's *right*," he said, smacking his head. "And as usual, you've made a terrific point."

As we approached the top of the mountain, we saw a crowd of monkeys following us along below, chattering and baring their teeth and taking swipes in our direction as if they were trying to get at us. I thought it was a clever touch on the part of the Japanese to arrange it so that we could watch the monkeys carry on in a threatening manner yet remain beyond their reach. But we did not stay that way for long. As we touched down, the monkeys were on hand to greet us, spitting and screeching and continuing to take those nasty swipes in our direction. Signs were posted saying that visitors were not to annoy the monkeys, which struck me as being ironic since *they* were the ones who were trying to get at us.

We shooed them off to the best of our ability and made our way across a primitive rope bridge and then on to a large clearing in the woods where we saw an amazing sight.

A long line of workers in fatigues paraded by us carrying inflatable penises of all shapes and sizes. Some were erect while

others were in a more relaxed state and had ribbons tied
around them at the base of the scrotum. A float accompanied
the marchers, carrying a band that played, "Straighten Up and
Fly Right" and then segued into, "Baby, Won't You Light My
Fire."

Groups of family members lined the parade route carrying
souvenir penises of their own and waving them supportively at
the marching breadwinners. The atmosphere was that of a festival, and I would have settled in to enjoy it had I not been sad-
dled with an onerous responsibility.

Concession stands at the edge of the woods did a banner
business selling ice cream in the shape of penis shafts, each
adorned with two small scoops at the base to suggest testicles—a
touch that I personally felt was in poor taste and bordered on
the tacky. There were also foot-long hotdogs for sale, which
made their point without having to be tarted up.

Though most of the crowd had joined in the spirit of the
event, a small but vociferous group of women held up inflatable
vaginas and carried signs in both English and Japanese that said:
WHAT ABOUT US? and HOW LONG, OH LORD, HOW LONG?

I had never seen anything like it—and that was putting it
mildly. But as I watched the parade go by, I recalled an evening
at a campfire site—long before—in the company of Little Irwin
and his father, Little Irwin Sr., who was a rascal in his own right.
Little Irwin and I sat at Little Irwin Sr.'s feet and listened in
fascination as he described to us a similar event (though on a
smaller scale) he had accidentally happened upon in Hokkaido,
as a member of the occupation forces in postwar Japan. Needless to say, we hung on his every word.

"I almost got my ass shot off when they spotted me," he
had said, "but it was the highlight of my wartime experience."

So obviously this was not a one-shot; the event appeared to
be part of a tradition, albeit one the Japanese people did not
care to publicize. And judging from the suspicious looks that
came our way, they were no more eager to have the event wit-

nessed by outsiders than they were when Little Irwin Sr. had been a GI.

I personally did not see what they were being so touchy about. In other societies, everything from broomsticks to baseball bats are interpreted as being penis symbols. The Japanese people had cut through all of that to declare their respect and admiration for the penis *itself.* Shouldn't they be given credit for being forthright? That's the way *I* would vote—and I made a mental note to mention the event in a letter to my Montagnard friends. Since they lived their lives in a more natural state than the rest of us, they would be sure to appreciate it.

"JESUS CHRIST," SAID Kevin, smacking his head and ignoring the female protestors. "Did you ever see so many cocks in your life! It's a lucky thing Sandy isn't here. She would have been *very* upset."

"It's not that arousing," I said.

"Really? All those peckers are not that *arousing*? I don't know about you, but I am getting *very* hot."

He thought a second and said: "That doesn't make me a fag, does it?"

"A gay guy," I said, politically correcting him. "And I doubt it."

Just then, a huge float sailed by carrying a small man in a business suit who sat astride a huge flower-bedecked penis, the most prominent one in the parade. He waved at the cheering crowd and judging from their reaction, I could only assume that the neatly dressed executive was Mr. Matsumoto. Though I was only able to get a quick look at him, it seemed to me that he was a bit young to have been a contemporary of the octogenarian Thomas Gnu. I had felt the same way about Dickie Moué and ended up ascribing his youthful appearance to some quirk related to his illness. Here again, it was possible that Mr. Matsumoto's well-preserved appearance was a result of his having led an exemplary life (notwithstanding his unwillingness to sleep with the same woman more than once).

Then, too, it is difficult for me to judge the age of the Japanese people, as I would imagine it is hard for them to judge ours.

We got some more hostile looks from the crowd, no doubt because of our Western appearance, mine in particular, that caused us to stand out. To help us blend in, we bought some souvenir penises of our own and joined the crowd in waving them at the workers as they filed by. The tempo of the event picked up when a trio of clowns came tumbling out of a fire truck and delighted the crowd by setting off exploding penises. A group of marchers wearing John Wayne masks sauntered by with Stetsons on their penises, carrying signs that said: BIG SWING-ING DICKS.

At one point, an enthusiastic marcher got carried away and laughingly whipped out his own penis, pointing it at the crowd. The waggish fellow was immediately seized by security guards and hustled off the parade grounds while the crowd whistled and hooted its disapproval. But obviously, flagrant displays of sexuality were not about to be tolerated.

Kevin poked me in the side and drew my attention to a befuddled little band of Tony Bennett fans who held aloft pictures of the celebrated ballad singer and had obviously wandered into the wrong parade.

"Wait till I tell Sandy," he said excitedly. "She loves that guy."

I said I had great admiration for the venerable recording artist as well, but in truth, my thoughts were on Mr. Matsumoto and how to get him off by himself, an impossibility, it seemed, in the light of all the merrymakers who were milling about the parade grounds.

A partial solution presented itself when a siren went off and the marchers came to a halt. Picnic baskets were brought forth by family members and everyone settled in for a lunch break.

Up ahead, I could see Matsumoto's float veer off and come to a stop at a clearing in the woods. Several executives jumped down from the float and assisted Mr. Matsumoto as he slid gracefully down from his penis.

Kevin and I drew close and watched the executives set up a rustic banquet table and then call up to some underlings on the float. They quickly gathered up a number of freezer packs labeled SUSHI, and carried them down to be laid out on the table.

The sun had gone down. Since the opportunity we sought had not fully presented itself, Kevin and I decided to take a lunch break of our own. We found a quiet spot in the shade of some pine trees and broke out the tuna salad sandwiches and pickled vegetables that had been so thoughtfully provided by Sandy.

Before we had taken our first bite, a fireworks display started up, as if for our own personal enjoyment. Most were of a variety that I recognized, such as pinwheels and Roman candles. But others were not familiar to me. In the spirit of the event, they were shaped like penises. And if that were not novelty enough, they gradually grew in size, hit their zenith—and finally spurted off into the clouds, in simulation of the ejaculative function.

"That did it," said Kevin as he watched the display. "I'm whacking off."

"Suit yourself," I said. "But remember what happened to that fellow they dragged out of the parade."

"All right," said Kevin, backing off. "But there are hot guys out here, and they should have taken that into account. Not that I want to say anything against my people."

Despite their erotic nature, the fireworks had no effect on me other than to sharpen my concentration. I studied Mr. Matsumoto as he enjoyed his sushi lunch, passing up the traditional chopsticks in favor of a knife and fork. No doubt this was an accommodation he had made to the Western CEOs he was forced to deal with.

Taking advantage of our concealed position, I started to attach the silencer to my weapon. But I must have been a bit more jittery than I realized, and in fumbling around, I shot off a round that caused the earth around us to shake.

"Jesus Christ," said Kevin, as he covered his ears and dove for cover. "What was *that?*"

"It was unintentional," I said, fearing that we would immediately be apprehended. But as luck would have it, the discharge was covered by the sound of the exploding penis fireworks. Several of the marchers did look over at us suspiciously, but then one of them smiled and applauded lightly, having assumed that we had joined in on the festivities with some modest fireworks of our own.

"I don't want to insult you," said Kevin. "You're a great guy, and you made a terrific impression on Sandy, but are you *sure* you know what the fuck you're doing?"

"Trust me," I said, affecting a steely eyed gaze and a confident look.

"That's some look," said Kevin, drawing back defensively and throwing up his hands. "You just scared the hell out of me."

"Good."

At that point, Mr. Matsumoto stood up, bowed to his executive assistants and excused himself from the table.

"This is it," I said as I watched him start off toward the woods, no doubt to relieve himself.

There was no question his company had the resources to provide him with a portable commode, but he had obviously spurned it because of his democratic nature—and perhaps as a cost-cutting measure.

"Good luck," said Kevin. "I'd help you, but I'm very nervous and you're probably getting paid more than I am. Not that you have to tell me the exact figure unless you want to."

I let the question go unanswered and started forward toward the woods, surprised at how relaxed and focused I was. Though I had gone through considerable inner turmoil before signing on for the venture, I had experienced very little since. Did that mean I was cold and insensitive? I doubt it—but will leave it for others to decide.

Matsumoto poked his way through the brambles, found a spot to his liking and unzipped his trousers. Drawing on a technique I recalled from my days in the armed forces, I lined him up in my sights, took a deep breath and held it. As I was about to pull the trigger, half a dozen hooded men dropped down from the trees, surrounded Matsumoto and began to whack him about the head with long black penis-like objects. At first I thought it might be part of the celebration, but the heavy dull sound of the blows led me to believe that the penises in use were of a lethal variety. Mr. Matsumoto fell to the ground, and after finishing him off with additional blows to the head, the hooded intruders disappeared in the woods.

Who were these uninvited Ninja-style thugs, I had to wonder. Was it possible that Peabody had lost confidence in my abilities at the last minute and signed them up to do the job for me? If that were so, I would have been sorely disappointed.

And did this unexpected turn of events mean that I would not get paid?

Setting aside these troubling concerns for the moment—and acting out of some ineradicable humanistic impulse, I rushed forward to help the man but quickly saw that I had arrived too late. Kevin had followed close behind me and drew back in horror when he saw the slain executive.

"Jesus Christ," he said, stifling a near hysterical laugh. "They beat him to death with *schvonces.*

"I'm sorry, Matthew," he said, realizing his comment may have come across as unfeeling. "But isn't that what happened?"

Selfishly, and to my everlasting shame, I thought of giving

the poor man a few taps with my souvenir penis so I could claim that, at least technically, I had been in on his demise.

But I could not bring myself to go to such lengths.

A group of executive assistants soon appeared on the site. When they saw Mr. Matsumoto's lifeless form, they fell to their knees, pounded at the ground with their fists, and emitted deep-throated guttural moans that were distinctly different in type from our American mourning sounds. One of the executives managed to pull himself together long enough to ask what had happened. Since I had only a meager knowledge of the Japanese language, I deferred to Kevin, who filled him in, and then pointed to the area of woods through which the intruders had made their escape. Several security guards showed up, and when the situation had been explained to them, they set off through the woods in pursuit of the perpetrators. By that time a huge crowd had gathered and proceeded to express their grief over the loss of their beloved employer.

Since no one had thought to detain us—Kevin and I quietly made our exit from the parade grounds.

Chapter Twelve

P EABODY SPOKE IN a strangled voice, as if his mouth were filled with hot potatoes.

"Now look here, Binny. I've reviewed that chicken project of yours, and I'm more convinced than ever that it's not right for me. Let me assure you that my feelings have nothing to do with merit. As a matter of fact, I find the second stage of your procedure quite intriguing. But I know my capabilities, and I wouldn't have the faintest idea of how to proceed with it."

"I always felt the second stage is the one that needs work."

"No, no, you're wrong on that. The second stage is ingenious. I really got into it when I reached the second stage. But ultimately, it's not for me. More to the point, you're a darling man. I adore working with you and can hardly wait to see you. When do you leave?"

"On the first available plane."

It was amazing. I had called Peabody from Japan to explain what had happened on the parade grounds and all he wanted to talk about was my procedure for eliminating northern fowl mites from caged layer hens. It was as if he had thought of nothing else since I'd left. Surprisingly, he hadn't heard of the attack on Mr. Matsumoto, but as I filled him in on the details, he listened with little interest as if his mind was on larger issues.

"You didn't happen to hire those fellows, did you?" I asked.

"Of course not, Binny. I'm surprised at you."

Then, *not* surprisingly, he told me I could forget about the $250,000 fee I was supposed to receive. As to the money I owed the organization, he said I should just relax; he was sure they would make some kind of "arrangement."

Reduced down to basics, what this meant as I prepared to leave Japan was that I was now some $50,000 in the hole. I tried to think of some good that had come out of the experience and consoled myself with the thought that I had at least been among the Japanese and had a sense of their way of doing things, which was so different from ours and easily accounted for the conflicts that kept springing up between our two great nations.

As an example, they were ashamed of almost everything they did—yet they went ahead and did it. Whereas if we were ashamed of some action of ours, we might think twice before proceeding. That type of thing.

Naturally, I would have preferred to stay a bit longer so that I could visit a few shrines and maybe catch one of their puppet shows. But as always, I was anxious to get back to Lettie.

I HAD A last drink with Kevin Kurosawa at the hotel and told him it looked like I would not get paid for all that work.

"I understand your feelings, Matthew, and believe me I feel for you. You're hurt and I don't blame you. But look at it this way. You've got your health, you've got your family, although it *is* tragic that you lost your wife, and believe me I feel for you on that, too—but the important thing is that you *tried,* which is all anyone can expect. *I* tried to make the networks, I came *this* close; there were certain people who were out to get me, but I did try. If you like, I'll call Val and tell him you're a credit to his organization. If you ask me—and I'm sure Sandy would agree—he should kiss your ass in appreciation of the job you're doing."

"I don't need him to kiss my ass."

"That's your decision, Matthew, and I respect it. I'd also like to add that you made a terrific impression on the guys at the Parrot Club. They expected you to be a snob, but you came across as a modest guy and charmed the shit out of them."

"Maybe I'll come back and actually spend some time with them."

"I wouldn't do that. Sometimes it doesn't work out the

second time. You do have some flaws, you *are* a little sensitive. They might notice that on a repeat visit. I'd quit while I was ahead.

"Take care of yourself," he said, giving me a farewell hug. "And if you happen to run into someone at one of the networks, I'd appreciate your putting in a good word for me. I can announce, Matthew. *Believe* me. All I need is a break."

Though it was unlikely that I'd meet any network representatives in our community, I said that if I ran into one I would certainly tell the fellow about Kevin. Upon hearing that, he became emotional, and it was all I could do to get him out of the hotel before he collapsed in tears. Yet there was no question that I had made a new friend, whether I wanted one or not. A friend who would be there if I ever got into trouble, which I was in already.

Not that anyone would ever take the place of Little Irwin.

After seeing Kevin off, I returned to the lobby, and picked up an English-language newspaper, which reported in a front-page story that the police had apprehended the men who had attacked Mr. Matsumoto at the penis festival. They were identified as a group of turbine grinders who had become incensed when the work they did at the Matsumoto Company was farmed out to a shop in Queens that claimed it could do the job for half the price. Though the accused men acknowledged that Mr. Matsumoto was a decent man and had probably acted in response to the rising yen, they felt they had to bash in his head in order to make a statement.

So Peabody had not despatched them, after all.

Impressed as I was by the speed and efficiency of the Japanese police, their excellent work did not help my situation. It could be argued that I was in worse shape than when I had started out for Japan. Certainly this was true of my finances. Yet oddly enough, I did not feel in the least bit dejected. As Kevin had astutely pointed out, I had worked up to the full limit of my capabilities. Was it my fault that fate had intervened and sent an incensed bunch of turbine grinders to carry out my assignment?

As Lettie would say: *I don't think so!*

Though I knew my daughter was too old for toys, I found one at the airport that I could not resist buying. It was a little Japanese fellow with a pointy hat and a pointy nose who would trot up to the side of the counter, look down, decide it was a bad idea to jump down, then turn around and somersault over to the other end of the counter to see what the situation was there. And so on. He was the most intelligent little mechanical fellow I had ever come across, one more example of Japanese ingenuity.

I'd hate to be around if they ever decided to start another war.

I took a last look around and then boarded the plane, anxious to see my daughter and to return to the country I would never forsake, which is not to say that I wouldn't consider returning to Japan for a couple of months if, for example, someone offered me a grant.

If nothing else, I could tell them about chickens.

Chapter Thirteen

LETTIE WAS WAITING for me with some questions she had stored up, and as usual they were hard ones.

She wanted to know about thunder and lightning. I took a stab at lightning, saying it had something to do with electricity in the clouds. As to thunder, the best I could come up with is that it followed lightning, which she knew. Then I got a little fancy and said that thunder might be the gods' way of roaring their approval of lightning. She wasn't so sure about that, but my speculation did lead her into inquiring about our family's position on God. I said we more or less believed in him, but only informally. The case that he existed was only circumstantial, but it was a strong one, as evidenced by the trees and the flowers and the freckles on her nose—which obviously didn't just get there.

And I made sure to say that for all we knew it could be a woman up there.

"I think it's a man. But what about the devil?"

"He's just there to balance things out so that we don't have too easy a time of it. And besides, he's fun."

"Why do bad things have to happen?"

"The best explanation I ever heard on that is that God is a novelist, and he has to think of exciting new plot developments to keep the story going. Sometimes he forgets that there are flesh and blood folks down here playing his characters and having to act out his scenes."

"Maybe he should have an assistant to remind him."

"I think he should. But he's probably on a tight budget."

I got a laugh out of her on that one.

Then she said: "I don't see why I have to go to school when I could stay home with you and learn just as much."

Though I was flattered by Lettie's confidence in me, I did

not feel there was much in the way of formal knowledge I could pass along to her. Inspired by my father's interest in literary matters, I had signed up at the local junior college for an English program, thinking there might be a place for me at some point in the burgeoning field of communications. But my hopes came crashing down when a substitute English teacher accused me of plagiarism in a book report. What I had written was that in 1940 "the black clouds of Nazi oppression hovered over a sleeping Europa."

"No freshman could come up with that," he had said, waving my paper in the air and embarrassing me in front of my classmates, several of whom happened to be cute girls. (One of them was *really* cute and kept crossing and uncrossing her legs, offering up a slice of panties, and driving me to distraction.) As a result of his attack on my integrity, I fainted and had to be slapped awake by the botany instructor.

I felt I had no choice but to leave school, even though the head of the department said I could continue if I was careful in the future about stealing other people's descriptive passages.

That ended my college studies—a classic case of a promising student (and let me blow my own horn here) cut down by a cruel and frivolous accusation. Who knows what heights I might have attained had I been permitted to continue at school. Should we put such power in the hands of mean-spirited so-called educators (no doubt with their own private agenda) who with a careless and unthinking whim can snuff out the dreams of a young man, be he gifted or not? (And why has no one in authority come forth to ask *that* question?)

Despite the setback, I continued along, and, of course, I soon developed expertise in poultry distribution. But beyond that, I could not honestly offer more to Lettie than scraps of information I had picked up along the way through my personal reading. I could recite a few lines of Shakespeare—"I can summon spirits from the vasty deep"—that type of thing—and I had some knowledge of historical figures, if not the forces that determined history itself. For example, I knew that Helmuth von Moltke had defeated the French in 1870 by using an ingenious railroad system that enabled him to get his troops to the front before the enemy arrived. I could also hold forth on the Schlieffen Plan and how the Germans, if they had paid strict attention to it, might have emerged victorious in the Great War. And of course there was my theory of the prostate gland and how it had affected historical decisions to a much greater degree than people realized.

So I could tell Lettie about von Moltke and Schlieffen and the prostate gland (I hadn't yet and was waiting for the proper time to salt all of that in), but I was aware that she would need much more in order to get ahead in life.

And of course there was another concern. Considering the work I had been doing for Peabody, could I claim to have the moral credentials to teach a young child? I'm not even going to touch that one.

"You're better off in school," I told her.

THEN WE GOT ready for dinner at Peabody's hotel. He had asked me to join him and said he'd be honored to have Lettie come along this time.

"Is it a dress-up affair?" she asked me.

"I don't see why not."

She raced into her room and took about forty seconds to get into her white party dress.

With her big brown eyes and her long brown hair, still wet from the shower, she looked like a young French girl from the Loire Valley or some place like that, waiting to be discovered as a Hollywood actress.

"You look beautiful."

"All fathers say that."

"I know they do. But I'm right."

Chapter
Fourteen

P EABODY GREETED ME as if he were standing on the White House lawn and I had just come back from a tough negotiation in the Middle East.

"Binny, Binny, Binny," he said, embracing me. "Welcome back. It's tremendously good to see you."

I said I was happy to see him, too, and the three of us sat down at the Garfield Hotel dining room table that he had reserved. There were chandeliers overhead, and the table was all set up with candelabras and long-stemmed wine glasses.

Lettie pulled her high-back chair in close and buried herself in the menu.

"She's ravishing," Peabody whispered to me, "but I don't think she much cares for me."

"She's shy," I whispered back, although he may have been right.

"You're too kind, Binny," he said, becoming disconsolate. "It's been that way all my life. Women showing some mild interest in me and then suddenly disappearing."

"It only takes one," I said, trying to cheer him up and thinking of all the dating I had done before I ran into Glo at the hog auction.

"It's too late," he said, looking mournfully off in the distance.

Then he had one of his sudden mood swings.

"Actually," he said brightly, "I'm having rather a decent time of it living alone."

And he did look pretty good, as if he'd spent a lot of time on a treadmill and possibly under a sunlamp.

When the waiter arrived, Lettie asked me if she could have the chicken and a glass of milk. She was aware of how sensitive I'd become about anything having to do with poultry since losing my job at the distributor. And she always made sure to check with me before ordering a chicken dish. But now that I had branched out into another field, I was much less touchy about the subject and told her to go right ahead with the chicken.

When our food arrived, I trimmed the fat off Lettie's portion of legs and thighs and then cut the breast into little pieces before sliding the plate back over to her.

Peabody acted as if it was the most amazing thing he had ever seen in his life.

"My God, Binny," he said, almost choking on his salad. "You're cutting up her *chicken*. Why on earth are you doing that?

"I'm not going to be able to do it much longer," I said. "So I might as well do it now."

"But don't you see . . ." he said, and then his voice trailed off as if my actions had been so outrageous that any attempt to comment on them would be hopeless.

Then he settled down and looked at the two of us fondly.

"You're so lucky, Binny. My family's a bloody mess. And you have your wife . . . daughter . . ."

"My wife is dead."

"Oh, yes, she is, isn't she. I believe you mentioned that. And now you'll probably never forgive me."

"I forgive you. But I do like to keep it straight."

"I can well appreciate that."

Then he turned his attention to Lettie.

"So, Lettie," he said brightly. "You're a chicken fancier, are you. So are my daughters, come to think of it."

Lettie nodded thoughtfully as if to absorb the fact that Peabody's daughters enjoyed chicken. He asked her if she liked school and swimming and things like that, and she gave him one-word answers such as "yes" and "no," which he responded to with a nervous giggle. I had probably told him that Lettie was interested in movie producing and he said he had various friends in London named Ian and Nigel who were in the film business, but he didn't get too far with her on that score either.

There was a children's arcade in the lobby, and when we had polished off our desserts, I gave her some quarters to go play in it.

"It isn't that she doesn't like me," said Peabody, when Lettie had left the table. "She hates me."

"It's nothing personal. She's the same way with me on the phone."

"Yes, but we're not *on* the phone," said Peabody despairingly.

We ordered brandies and after we had taken a few sips of them, Peabody beamed at me and said: "So here we are, old friend. I can't tell you what a pleasure it's been working with you. You've got a tremendous knack for this sort of thing, and it would be a pity if you dropped it."

"You mean we're finished?"

"Well, yes," he said, and then added wistfully, "although it does seem a bit incomplete, doesn't it?"

"For one thing, I didn't actually do anything."

"You mustn't feel that way. I certainly know what you've accomplished. I just wish Thomas Gnu was aware of it. I tried to get through to him and tell him about Dickie and Matsumoto, but he's closed his office and gone off to Uzbekistan to see some woman. Imagine traveling all that distance for a blowjob."

"You'd think he'd be able to get one closer to home."

"You'd have to know him. Dreadful little man," he shuddered. "But with regard to the work we've done, it's as if there's some ingredient missing in an otherwise excellent sauce. I can't quite put my finger on it, but if I do, I promise to be in touch."

"What about the money?" I asked.

"Oh, yes," he said, pulling a little packet out of his pocket and handing it to me. "Thanks for reminding me. I've given you a coupon book. You can mail something off to us each month. It doesn't have to be substantial. There's no need for you to put a strain on yourself. On the other hand, you don't want to avert our eyes, so to speak.

"And I'd better go now," he said, getting to his feet. "Say goodbye to Lettie for me. I'd stay a bit longer but I don't want to become too emotional."

AND THAT WAS that and for all I knew it might have been the last I'd ever see of Valentine Peabody.

When we got back to the house, I took a look at the coupon book and saw that there were about three years' worth of monthly payments that had to be made, with a penalty for being more than fifteen days late. The checks were to be made out to a company called Global Enterprises, Inc., and sent to a post office box in Karachi, Pakistan.

The first thing in the morning I wrote one out for $200 and mailed it off so I would not have to worry about it for a while. I still had around $25,000 left from my $85,000 advance and decided I would take the payments out of that for as long as it lasted. After that, they could just come and get me. Who knows, maybe they would be the first to get blood out of a stone.

And after all, I did have something on them, not that I liked to think that way.

Chapter
Fifteen

O DDLY ENOUGH, AS I faced an uncertain future, I did not feel in the least bit dispirited. My rich experiences in Miami Beach and Tokyo had given me a taste of life's possibilities.

For all I knew, there might be more to come.

As if in preparation, I busied myself with self-improvement and read the novels of the great Canadian, Robertson Davies. One of them addressed itself to the problems of aging and temporarily eased my fears about that phenomenon. I had never felt they had much going on in Canada, but having him up there for all those years was all they needed.

And one night, I attended a lecture by one of our own famous novelists at the Baptist Church. I sat next to a little girl who I took to be about thirteen and wondered why she was up so late—until I realized that she was an adult who happened to be on the extremely petite side. She took notes during the lecture, which led me to believe that she was a student at the community college that I had been forced to leave because of a trumped-up plagiarism charge. (Not that I held it against her personally.) Though we did not speak, we exchanged several pleasant smiles, and I was only too happy to let her have the armrest.

The famous novelist made the point that few people read serious novels anymore, but he was going to keep writing them anyway.

"It's too late to change," he said. "And what would I do, write screenplays? Would Beckett? Insult me not."

I could not help wondering who it was that kept badgering him to write screenplays. His agent? And why was he so dead set against it? Was it possible that he had made a few stealthy tries at that type of work and couldn't get the hang of it?

He proceeded to read from his least famous novel—one that the critics had scorned—although the audience, myself among them, would clearly have preferred that he read from his *most* famous novel, since it had cost fifteen dollars to get into the lecture.

After the reading, someone asked why he had chosen to read from a novel that frankly no one had ever heard of.

"One nurtures the sick pup," was his answer.

The little girl next to me took notes on that, and then someone asked him about the future of the planet, and he said that frankly he didn't care about it since he was seventy-four. That got a big laugh from the audience, but when he repeated himself a few times—"I really don't give a shit about the planet" were his exact words—the laughs petered out.

Finally, the superintendent of our school system got to his feet and with jowls quivering said he had a grandson and that he *did* care about the planet. That got a huge round of applause from the audience, which had obviously been waiting for someone to make that statement. The famous novelist shrank down in his seat a bit, although there was no sign that he had altered his views.

After the lecture, I exchanged some more smiles with the girl who sat beside me. Then I watched her walk off, bravely carrying a briefcase that was almost as big as she was. She was the littlest girl I had ever sat next to, and I felt there had been a connection between us. I thought about her all the way home, though obviously I should have been grappling with the ideas thrown off by the writer in his least famous novel. (If nothing else, to get my money's worth.) And that may have been the trouble with the novel, incidentally, too many ideas jockeying for attention while the story went out the window. (He was signing books at the church, and I was tempted to run back there and point that out—but I would probably be telling him something that he knew.)

IT'S POSSIBLE THAT I had developed a false sense of security, but I had plenty of cash, even if, strictly speaking, it wasn't mine. So money was not of paramount concern to me, although I did feel it was important to keep busy. Still, I did not have much of an appetite for returning to my part-time position of manning the timer at the tanning salon, even if it had been offered to me, which it hadn't been.

A pharmaceutical company had posted flyers around town calling for paid volunteers to test a new flavored arthritis pill, and I considered the offer, but backed down, thinking there might be some long-term effect on your system that they conveniently chose not to mention.

For all I knew, the pill might *give* you arthritis when you didn't have it.

There *was* one job opening in which you got to wear an apron and hand out free cups of coffee at the mall—and then tried to talk the people who accepted them into buying the coffeemaker. But there was a line around the block for that one, so I didn't even try for it.

As to the cottage, I became less and less enthusiastic about selling it. It was my foundation, and I thought it possible I might fall apart without it. When Little Irwin first saw the cottage, he had said, in a rare serious moment: "This is the house in which you will die."

That's the way I felt each time I sat out on the porch in the evening and looked out on Liar's Pond.

So I called the real estate agent and told her I had changed my mind and decided to take my house off the market. That is, unless I received a really big offer, which was unlikely. I expected her to say, "You never know," but she said she agreed with me wholeheartedly.

Still, I was happy I had made the call.

One day I went over to the bookstore to see if I could find a good true-crimer. Though I am not proud of it and generally prefer books that expand my horizons, once in a while I get in the mood for a juicy one that doesn't. It didn't take long for me to find a beauty! It had all the ingredients I enjoy, featuring as it did a golden-haired California couple whose affluent life, at least on the surface, seemed to be idyllic. He was a rising young executive in marketing who drove a Porsche, and she was active in community affairs and at the country club. Both were clean-limbed and attractive and had two kids (which is not the part I like).

Though they were obviously living over their heads, racking up all kinds of charges on credit cards, they seemed to have it all. Yet beating up against the surface of their supposedly perfect life (there has to be something beating up against the surface for me to enjoy this type of book), there lay a whole vortex of kinkiness and depravity. Some of the ingredients in that vortex were arson, blackmail, adultery, incest and tax evasion, to name but a few. And it all culminated in a brutal axe murder.

This was all described on the flyleaf.

There were also pictures of the couple when they had just gotten married and had the whole world at their fingertips— and others, taken later on, of the husband in police custody, handcuffed and looking gaunt and unshaven. (I try not to look at the pictures before I finish the book, but that's a tough assignment.)

Needless to say, the book had my name on it, and I could hardly wait to tear into it.

I was on my way to the counter to pay for it when I noticed a customer who looked familiar to me. Then I remembered why. She was the little girl who had sat beside me at the lecture in which the famous novelist said he didn't give a shit about the planet. You could hardly see her head above the New Arrivals counter, but it was unmistakeably her, since there weren't too many girls that short in our community. (Many are stocky about the legs because of their farm background, but of medium height.)

The fact that we had attended the same lecture at the Baptist Church gave me a perfect excuse to say hello and to see if I could get a conversation going. If she showed a lack of interest, it would hardly count as a rejection since she was so little. (I am not proud of that type of thinking, but what can I say.)

My fears, however, turned out to be unfounded.

"Sure I remember you," she said after I had introduced myself. "You were the one who asked about the planet."

"No, I didn't" I said, refusing to take credit for someone else's achievement. "But I wish I had."

"Oh," she said softly, and seemed a little disappointed that I was not the fellow who had asked the excellent question. But after we had paid for our books (she bought *Moo* and *Mistress to an Age: A Life of Madame de Staël*), we ended up having a cup of gourmet coffee together at the literary-style cafe next door. (To heighten the bookish atmosphere, there are pictures on the wall of Anais Nin and Kurt Vonnegut.)

She said her name was Beth and that she was indeed an English major at the junior college that I had to leave after being humiliated.

"I hope to be a teacher some day," she said.

I saw no reason to tell her that I was a contract killer, so I said I was between shows at the moment, and left it at that.

"At times like this, the only thing that keeps me going is a good book."

"You can say that again," she said.

She had soft brown hair, a pleasant face and a friendly easygoing style. In other words, her personality did not seem to have been adversely affected by her size. I got more and more interested in her and said that although I was somewhat tied to the house, I'd like to see her again. Evidently, and without knowing it, I had been anxious to have a simple and straightforward person in my life. I told her where I lived and maybe she could drop by sometime. She said that she would try.

I thought that was probably the last time I would see her.

191

Therefore I was pleasantly surprised one rainy afternoon when she knocked on my door. She wore a raincoat and carried a wet briefcase and had a career-oriented look about her.

"I finished up my classes early," she said, "and thought I'd drop by and pay you a visit."

I told her I was happy to see her and to come on in.

"All I was doing was reading that true-crimer book you saw me buy."

She took off her raincoat, sat down on the recliner, crossed her sturdy little legs and smiled at me.

"How did your books work out?" I asked.

"*Moo* was great, but I've been having trouble getting into *Mistress to an Age: A Life of Madame de Staël.*"

"Maybe it will pick up."

"I certainly hope so."

And with that, we seemed to run out of conversation.

I thought of asking her if she wanted a cup of coffee, but it didn't seem necessary. We just sat there, smiling at each other, as we had at the Baptist Church—and didn't exchange a word.

After a little more of that, I got up, took her hand, led her into my room and undressed her. It seemed like the most simple and straightforward thing in the world to do. She smiled throughout, as if she'd known all along that I had been curious about what it would be like to make love to a little person.

Little as she was, she was perfectly proportioned, except perhaps for her breasts, which were heavier than you would expect. (There they were again, those *unexpectedly* heavy breasts.) She also had perfect white skin and a clean powdery smell around her neck. And I could not help noticing that she had a rich profusion of ink-black pubic hair.

She let me twirl her overhead, which is something I had always wanted to do. (Glo would have been only too happy to oblige me, but her heftiness made it out of the question. And Cindy felt it was too close to her line of work as a stuntwoman.) Beth was light enough so that I could hold her upside down by the ankles and lower her up and down on my penis. And all she would do was chuckle. I thought it might be a tight squeeze—so to speak—down there, but that did not turn out to be the case. When I came inside her, she gave me the biggest hug, as if she appreciated my interest in making love to such a little person. I felt it was the other way around.

We held hands for a while and looked at the ceiling as lovers are apt to do. Then she got dressed, picked up her brief-case and we said goodbye.

Though clearly we had both enjoyed the experience, there was an unspoken agreement between us that there was no need to repeat it. For one thing, we looked ridiculous together. What she needed was someone closer to herself in size. It was a shame that Little Irwin was not around, although he was not bookish. (And all he ever cared about was one thing.)

Yet making love to that little watchfob of a girl was one of the most satisfying experiences I ever had. Why was that, I won-dered. I could hear some critic saying oh sure, she was little so you could control her. But if that was the case, how come I enjoyed making love to my wife from time to time (and may she rest in peace) when it would have taken a freight train to con-trol *her*. And couldn't it be argued that when Beth was up there being twirled, she was the one who was controlling me. Other-wise, why all that chuckling! So maybe it was just a case of two adults getting together on a rainy day and doing exactly what they wanted to do—which may not happen as often as we think.

At the same time, it was like a book you enjoy but know you will never read again. The way I felt about *And Silently Flows the Don*.

On the other hand, I just might give her a ring someday, to see how she was getting along.

IT DID CROSS my mind that my two romantic encounters—since becoming a widower—were with a bald girl and one who was height-challenged. (No disrespect to either one—both were fine individuals in their own way.) But would a normal-sized girl with a full head of hair ever come my way? I certainly hoped so.

Chapter
Sixteen

A S BRIEF AS it was, the affair with Beth put a little bounce in my step. And my good fortune continued. Out of nowhere, I received a call saying there was an opening at my old poultry company, although not in distribution. What they were looking for was an experienced de-beaker in the fast-growing turkey division. Additional responsibilities would include candling out infertile eggs in the hatchery and some de-snooding. Early in my career I had done some de-beaking, but I had never candled or de-snooded. Nonetheless I did not see why I could not pick up both techniques quickly, and I presented myself as being qualified. The work was a comedown from my previous position, but I was not about to stand on ceremony.

Each morning, after taking Lettie to school, I drove the Trooper out to the range, feeling that once again it was nice to have some place to go.

It had been some time since I had worked with turkeys, and I'd forgotten their unique traits. As an example, you must never back away from one. Should a Tom run up to you in a hostile manner—and they will always challenge a newcomer—it's important to hold your ground. Most of the time it will be the Tom who has second thoughts and will turn away. (We used to say the same thing about our enemies in the Pacific, and how wrong we were. But it *is* true of most turkeys.)

Once you've demonstrated that you are not afraid of turkeys—even if you secretly are—they will follow you around and get under your feet, which can be a nuisance. Another thing is that you can't get upset when the poults peck at each others eyes. It may seem barbaric, but it is just part of the turkey scene.

And you have to remember to dry them off quickly when it rains or they're liable to drop dead on you.

I had the range pretty much to myself except for two female co-workers. One was stocky and had close-cropped curly blonde hair and nicotine stains on her teeth. Her name was Edna. The other, Caroline, was dark and slender and much more feminine in style. She looked like an attractive librarian. They stuck together and held hands when they felt no one was looking, which led me to believe that they were a lesbian couple—not that it affected my feelings about them.

I did wonder, however, who it was that ran the show in these situations. I had heard that often, and surprisingly, it is the outwardly feminine one who has the upper hand. That seemed to be the case with these two. Every once in a while Edna would walk over to the fence and unaccountably start to cry. And Caroline would go over there and comfort her. And never once did I see the more sensitive-appearing Caroline break out into tears. So you never knew.

One day I made the mistake of asking Edna how long she had been a Poultry Maid. I almost got my head handed to me. Though the term had been in use since time immemorial, it no longer was, as I learned to my great discomfort. Hatchery Technician was the new designation, and as far as I was concerned, the change was long overdue.

After that one gaffe, we all became friends and worked together as a team on our one day a week in the slaughterhouse. That demonstrated to me that people of all kinds can get along if they will only learn not to pry into each other's personal affairs.

I have no use for those talk shows in which they do.

ONE NIGHT, MY new friends invited me to have dinner at a road-house restaurant that specialized in vegetarian-style food, which does not happen to be a favorite of mine. But I went along anyway, just to be in their excellent company. The restaurant was called Fran's, and it appeared to cater to lesbian types. There were half a dozen such couples sitting around who seemed to fit that description, although you have to be careful here. Just because two women are holding hands and having a cozy candlelit dinner, you can't jump to the conclusion that they are lesbians. Yet the ones I was looking at probably were. We listened to some country music on the jukebox, which was probably lesbian-slanted but that someone like myself who is not a lesbian could enjoy all the same. Since I was out of my depth in a restaurant of that type, I let my friends do the ordering. They asked for a variety of tofu dishes that weren't half as bad as I thought they'd be. I noticed that some of the couples had brought along their own little bags of nuts and berries, as if they didn't trust the restaurant food to be natural enough. But the mood was casual and the restaurant didn't seem to mind.

During dinner, Edna and Caroline confided in me that they were indeed lesbians.

"It's an honor for me to hear that," I said.

Then they told me about the troubles they had and how hard it was for them to find a place to stay when they were traveling, except for Greece. But they didn't want to keep going back and forth to Greece, and I couldn't blame them. Edna showed me a special lesbian magazine that addressed these very problems, giving its readers a list of inns where they could probably get in. There were also heartbreaking personal ads sent in by lonely lesbians who were seeking other lesbians who were just as lonely and wanted to get together for mountain climbing and things like that. I said I wouldn't mind subscribing to a magazine of that type, although in truth I had a feeling my interest would taper off after a few issues.

As we were about to start our dessert course, the Grimble brothers showed up, and I could tell they were looking for trouble. Otherwise, why would they frequent a vegetarian/lesbian roadhouse. They had probably been drinking, which is not to say their manners would have been impeccable if they hadn't. They didn't even bother to sit down at a table and pretend they'd come in for vegetarian dinners.

"Hey, Candy Ass," Myron called out to me. "Out with the boys tonight?"

His brother Vernon got hysterical as if it was the funniest thing he had ever heard. But I did not. If there's one thing I can't stand it's being called Candy Ass. Added to which he had insulted my two new friends by referring to them as "boys." I felt I had no choice but to fight them, knowing full well that no one had ever been able to defeat both Grimbles at once. (You could do all right if you got Myron off by himself, but that was about it.)

When I started to get up, Edna restrained me with a gentle hand on my shoulder. She then motioned to Caroline who stood up, lifted her chair and held it out horizontally toward her friend. Edna did some spins to get up momentum and then drove her fist through the heavily reinforced oaken seat.

If Myron was impressed by her performance, he took great pains not to show it.

"That's nothing," he said, taking a seat at our table. "And let me take a taste of that shit."

With that, he stuck a finger in Caroline's tofu pudding.

He was licking the finger daintily, making fake sounds of enjoyment, when Caroline reached across the table, grabbed his trachea, yanked him out of his chair and brought him face down on the Spanish tile.

Though I was no supporter of the surly Grimbles, I got sick to my stomach at the display of raw animalistic violence.

If I had to bet, I would have guessed that Vernon would come to his brother's aid, but he, too, must have been taken aback by Caroline's swift and unorthodox move.

"Hey, hey," he said, raising his hands defensively, and jumping up and down like a demented cheerleader. "All right, all right . . . just give me a minute to drag Myron out of here."

Which is what he did. And then we all went back to eating our desserts (after replacing the tofu pudding that Myron had stuck his finger in), just as if nothing out of the ordinary had happened. For the rest of the evening, Edna and Caroline regaled me with stories of the backstage hijinks they had witnessed as members of a gypsy dance troupe in outer Gdansk. And if there's one thing I learned from the experience, it's that you do not fuck with folks who practice an alternative lifestyle, no matter how mild-mannered they might appear to be.

ALL IN ALL, my job at the range made for a rewarding and healthful existence. Many turkeys are roamers and will bust out of the range and have to be tracked down. Chasing after them is a workout in itself, since there are Toms that can outrun a pickup. We received a decent wage and got to take home leftover Butterballs, so long as we didn't overdo it. I grew to love turkeys and signed a petition that said they should be designated as the national bird, which only seemed fair. As Edna pointed out to me, the turkey had been on the continent long before the bald eagle. Opponents of the switchover had always known that, but had felt that we didn't want to be known as a "turkey" of a nation.

My personal opinion is that it is the way we feel about ourselves that counts. Any country that thinks otherwise is the *real* turkey.

Chapter
Seventeen

I MAILED OFF another check to Global Enterprises, Inc., for $300 this time, which was only fair since I was employed now and had a small cash flow. That left a deficit of less than $60,000, which did not particularly worry me since they had not bugged me about it. And if they did, I'd be ready for them.

Naturally I thought about Peabody and what he was up to. My guess was that he was off in Rawalpindi working with that other fellow he had once felt was as good as I was. And I confess that I was a little jealous.

One day, on my lunch hour, I drove over to his old office and found the half-completed high-rise boarded up with a sign out front saying it had been reclaimed by a government agency. At the diner I asked Ed Bivens if he had heard from Peabody, and he responded by hitching up his pants, scratching his head and looking off in the distance.

"Oh, yeah," he said as if he had difficulty remembering him.

Then he quickly switched over to a trip his wife was forcing him to take to see her family in Nicaragua, all of whom had been opposed to their marriage.

"I just can't seem to win them over," he said with a sigh.

Betty, who could hear a leaf drop in the next county, looked up from the grill and gave him a sharp look.

"Maybe if you sent them a credit card and money they would learn to like you."

"I don't *have* any money to send," said Ed.

"Oh yes, you do, you sneak. Don't try to fool me."

Considering the way they fought, it was a miracle they were able to stay together. Yet that squabbling might have been the glue that kept them going.

* * *

So IT WAS as if Peabody had never existed. And then one day, just as his memory was starting to fade away on me like an old snapshot, I heard from him.

I had taken Lettie to the ballpark for a game in which our town was playing an all-black team from Shreveport. We only had three black ballplayers, but they were our best.

It was a picture-perfect day. The grass was bright green, the air was fresh and clear, and the sky looked as if someone had painted it a perfect blue. Everything looked so much more vivid than it did on TV, and it made you wish they had never invented the medium.

The attendants were all skinny high-school girls with straw-colored hair who wore sweatshirts and short skirts and who showed you to your seats. Then they hung around to take care of any special needs you might have. Each one seemed languid and distracted as if she was dreaming of the big city.

When the game began, two fellows behind third base started hollering out catcalls of an old-fashioned and benign nature such as "throw the bum out." Our players were excellent for the most part, but they were no match for the visitors from Shreveport, each of whom seemed good enough to qualify for the big leagues.

I spent as much time enjoying the tableau itself as I did watching the game. It was as all-American a phenomenon as I could imagine. Other countries might try to import our national pastime, but they will never capture its flavor, although they are welcome to try.

All this from someone who doesn't really care for the sport that much. My own preference is boxing, which is mano a mano and features nonstop action.

I'm not sure how much Lettie enjoyed the game. She is a player and not a watcher—but we were together and that's what counted. Along with the rest of the crowd, we got to our feet to stretch out before the start of the seventh inning, and Lettie wondered why we had to wait that long to do it. I said you could get up and stretch anytime you liked, but it was a baseball tradition that everybody did it together in the seventh inning. I wasn't sure why.

And then I heard my name being paged over the public address system.

"William Binny, please report to the front office. That's William Binny. Report to the front office, please."

"Maybe it's Hollywood," said Lettie, who had continued to pursue her goal of becoming a movie producer.

"Why would they want me?"

"Maybe they're doing a turkey movie."

"I doubt it."

I hesitated before leaving Lettie alone, but then I realized that we were surrounded by wholesome families who would see to it that she was nice and safe. So I told her I'd be right back and then made my way through the stands, embarrassed about the stir that I had created.

The front office was filled with baseball memorabilia, and I was all wedged in by pennants and souvenir bats when I took the call.

"Binny," said the voice at the other end, which I recognized as belonging to Peabody. "I'm not interrupting you, am I?"

"No, I was just watching a ballgame."

"You are?" he said. "They didn't tell me that. Who's winning?"

"Shreveport, but it's not important. It's just a thing to do."

"I'll just take a minute. Something's come up that might be just right for you. Thomas Gnu would like to do a couple this time, and the exciting thing is that they're in New York City. It's an opportunity for us to work together since I plan to be there. That's what I've always felt was missing, the two of us combining our efforts instead of you off somewhere at work and me sitting around twiddling my thumbs. The great news is that I've gotten Gnu to forgive your debt and to toss in a new $50,000 advance against the quarter-of-a-million completion fee. He's a cheap bastard, and he really surprised me, which leads me to believe that he wants this badly. How does it all sound?"

"I just started a new job," I said, not wanting to appear too eager.

"Really? Doing what?"

"De-beaking and de-snooding turkeys."

"I see. Sounds fascinating. I've been off writing poetry in Valparaiso myself. But do see if you can get out of the turkey thing. I'll send you a packet with everything you need.

"This is *it*, Binny, I can feel it. *Yes-s-s-s!* Oh, and one more thing."

"What's that?"

"My cholesterol has gone down to 190. Isn't that lovely?"

Chapter
Eighteen

WE FINISHED UP watching the game, although, as usual, Peabody had gotten me stirred up, making it difficult for me to concentrate. The part about forgiving my debt was appealing to say the least, and the extra $50,000 did not hurt either. With that kind of money, plus the twenty or so I had in the bank, I could sail right through until I reached the age of Social Security—and then I would be home free. I realized, of course, that it was only an advance—but there was something about *having* it in your possession.

Then, too, there was the chance to see the great city of New York, which I had somehow managed never to have visited. I did have a brief stopover in nearby Jersey City during my service years, but how could you compare the two.

I had some concern about the crime rate, but I had read an item saying that the new administration had cut into it—so maybe I would be lucky enough not to run into any.

And that was really something. *Me* concerned about the crime rate!

On the down side, Peabody said we'd be going after a couple, which seemed like twice the work. But to look at it another way, couples tended to stick together, so it might not be much different from my other ventures. Another concern was that I would have to give up my job on the turkey range; having left the poultry field once before, the chances were slim I would ever be hired back. They don't look approvingly on people who come and go—and who can blame them?

But finally, it was not much of a decision. My ego was such that I wanted to see just one of my assignments through to completion. And to show Peabody I was just as good as that hotshot in Rawalpindi he kept raving about.

I received a FedEx the next morning, clear evidence that

Peabody never doubted for a minute that I would get on board. It contained my itinerary and travel documents and that heavy bricklike packet that I did not even have to open, since I knew by now what it would contain. There was also a memo stating that an apartment in a "secure" building had been set aside for my use—and there were instructions on where to find the key— which was on the fifth floor and taped discreetly to the top of the mail chute.

You would have thought I had signed on with the CIA.

The big surprise was that there was an airline ticket for Lettie.

When I asked her how she felt about going to New York City, she responded with high excitement.

"That's great," she said. "The William Morris Agency is located there. I can go up to see them and get started on my career as a movie producer."

I saw no reason to tell her it was unlikely she could get an appointment with them and that she was far too young to get into movie producing. Why trample on a daughter's dream? So I let it go, and we made preparations for our trip. In one way, it was a blessing, since her school was in recess, and I had not been able to come up with any entertaining activities for her, other than having her accompany me to the turkey range, which would not have been much fun.

Peabody had arranged for me and Lettie to have two days together in the city before his arrival. There had been no men- tion of weaponry, so I brought along my powered Super V Tur- key De-beaker, just so I would have *something*.

The plane trip was uneventful, which was fine with me. We did get excited when the pilot dipped his wings and we got to circle LaGuardia Airport, affording us a view of the New York City skyline that had thrilled so many millions before us. I would have been content to circle around a few more times so I could feel the full effect of this majestic city.

The cab driver who took us into the city proper was of

Asian descent, and I was tempted to share my recent experiences in Tokyo with him. But on second thought, I decided it would be prudent to keep a low profile. I had heard horror stories of out-of-towners such as Lettie and myself being bilked by unscrupulous cab drivers, and the $150 fare did seem a bit high. But not when you considered there were two of us, it was a long ride in, and we were in the greatest city on earth.

The driver dropped us off in a quiet leafy area that was lined for the most part with townhouses and looked more like the way I imagined London to be than New York City. Our building was seven stories high and covered with ivy, which helped it blend right in with the townhouses. (I found out later that we were in Gramercy Park.)

Lettie and I had fun finding our key, which was exactly where it was supposed to be. The building was a quiet one and the only tenant we saw was an old lady with a veil who slipped past us as if we weren't there. And our apartment was a nice surprise. It had much more character than the one I'd been assigned to on the Dickie Moué caper. Though it was only partially furnished, there were antique sofas and couches in the living room, luxurious carpets and paintings on the wall that I identified as being in the French Impressionist style. It would not have surprised me to learn they were originals. There were two bedrooms, one of which featured a canopied bed with a little staircase beside it that you had to climb to get up there. I had my eye on it, but Lettie beat me to it, and I did not have the heart to say no to her. (When had I ever?)

The second bedroom was more of a utility space. It was stuffy and filled with file boxes and office-type equipment. But there was a foldout sofabed that would certainly get me by. Lettie had opened the closet of her bedroom and called me in to see what was in there. Piles of angora sweaters of every color were stacked up to the ceiling, and there were about forty dark suits on hangers. I checked the label on one, which said it had been made in Hong Kong.

All in all, the apartment smacked of wealth—on a global scale. It looked like some spoiled rich fellow had moved in, started to decorate it and then lost interest and moved out. A fellow so rich he could afford to leave everything behind.

While Lettie was trying out the canopied bed, I took a minute to light up a small cigar and to check the view from the living-room window. The apartment looked out on a beautiful well-maintained park with no one inside it. But there were people of every age and description, wearing shorts and bandannas and jogging around the park to try to get in shape. I sat down to rest my knee, and, as if I had ordered it up, I noticed a circular rack that held fifty different kinds of canes and walking sticks, one more beautifully crafted than the other. I pulled out an artistically gnarled-looking one and limped around the living room to try it out.

I was hoping Lettie would take a nap, but she was too revved up to even consider it, so we decided to get right on the case and explore the city. We are both pretty good walkers so we chose to do so on foot. I put my arm around Lettie's shoulders, because of the crime rate, but the people in our immediate neighborhood were so friendly that I soon saw it wasn't necessary. Many had a scholarly look about them and might have been professors. The men tipped their hats at us, and the women went out of their way to smile in our direction, making us feel right at home.

Of course, that could have been because we were a father and daughter, which appeals to everybody.

As we got deeper into the heart of the city, the people seemed to get more agitated, many of them bumping into each other without stopping to apologize. But that could have been because they were all crowded together and in a rush to get somewhere. I caught one fellow on a street corner leering at us as we walked by, but here again that could have happened in any major city. Still, I put my arm back around Lettie's shoulders as a precautionary measure.

What Lettie and I enjoyed most is the way the neighborhoods suddenly changed, as if you were in a theatre and the minute one play was over, the scenery was replaced to make way for another. We would be walking through an area that featured the sights and smells of India and just as we were starting to enjoy ourselves, it would end without warning and we would find ourselves on a street that looked like downtown Korea. And then boom, we would come upon a crowded street that was lined with jewelry stores and have to hurry to get out of the way of Hasidic gentlemen who were rushing in and out of them.

What we discovered is that New York is not one city but fifty of them rolled into one.

When we tired of all the excitement, we decided to eat some lunch and ducked into the first restaurant we could find that featured Italian cuisine. There were only a few people seated at the tables, and the place seemed to have fallen on hard times. After our linguini dishes had arrived, Lettie asked the waitress if any famous people ever ate there, and she said that Telly Savalas had once been a customer but that he had died.

"Would you like to see where Telly sat?" she asked.

Lettie said that wasn't necessary, just knowing that he was a customer was enough for her. But I knew she was just being polite and had been hoping that someone even more famous than Telly Savalas had eaten there—so that she could tell her girlfriends about it. (No disrespect to the great star of the long-running show, "Kojak," but Lettie was not of his generation.)

Withitall, the food was excellent and we couldn't understand why the restaurant wasn't more popular. When the waitress brought us our check, she furnished us with a possible explanation.

"Don't tell anyone I said this," she whispered, "but the owner died last year and the new one doesn't have much personality."

We were sorry to hear that. But as far as we were concerned, Tino's was still the restaurant to beat in New York City.

We also paid a visit to Macy's department store, which I found exhausting, although Lettie would still be racing up and down the aisles if I hadn't pulled her out of there. Then we went to the fabled F.A.O. Schwarz toy store, where Lettie bought a stuffed cat that was made in Taiwan and had more life to it than the real ones we had back home.

No trip to New York City would be complete without a visit to the Empire State Building, so naturally we headed over there. It impressed us, even though some loudmouth in the elevator spoiled things by telling everyone they were erecting a taller building in Jakarta, Indonesia.

I almost popped him one, but I knew that Lettie abhorred violence.

By the time we returned to our apartment, we were happily exhausted, and it was all we could do to kick back and watch some TV. Lettie tuned in to a sitcom on the living room set while I stretched out in the utility room and caught an excellent documentary on tics in Poland.

Then it was time for bed. I tucked Lettie in tight so that she wouldn't fall off the canopy bed in the middle of the night, and then I prepared to retire myself. It was hard finding a place for myself with the file folders spilling out onto the foldup bed. But once I was comfortable, I could not resist taking a peek at the contents of one of them. (It wasn't as if they were under lock and key.)

There were the usual prospectuses from Global Enterprises, Inc., offering deals in Europe that took advantage of tax loopholes and promised subscribers twenty times their investment in twenty minutes. But I also came across a brochure listing the upcoming schedule of a Jewish repertory theatre group in New Jersey. I was aware of the great contributions the Jewish people had made to the American stage (*Fiddler on the Roof* being a favorite of mine), and I was curious to see what this Jersey group was up to. They had a tasty variety of offerings scheduled, including an evening of Klezmer music, which I was not familiar with—and some one-act plays based on the writings of the esteemed novelist and vegetarian I.B. Singer, whose *Gimpel the Fool* I once had the pleasure of perusing. I could easily see myself sitting through either program, although we probably wouldn't have the time to get out there.

There was a page missing in the brochure—and I checked the table of contents to see what it was for. Evidently, it was supposed to show a picture of the theatre's artistic director. Out of curiosity, I looked at another brochure, a duplicate of the first, which *did* show his picture, and I received quite a surprise. Unless I was mistaken, the fellow in the photograph was the exact spitting image of Thomas Gnu, as represented in the slide projection I had seen in Peabody's office. The same mean little simian face, the mop of black hair that probably wasn't his, even the black turtleneck and black jacket. It may have been my imagination—after all, it had been several months since I saw the slide—but the resemblance was remarkable. Of course it was possible that the billionaire had an identical twin brother who had chosen to forsake the world of finance and go to work in the Jewish theatre of New Jersey.

Such occurrences are rare, but not unheard of.

Whatever the case, I decided to file this information away in my mind for future reference.

THE NEXT MORNING we had breakfast at a bagel shop, conveniently located just around the corner from our building—and I presented Lettie with a proposed agenda for the day: The Indian Museum; the dinosaur exhibit at the Museum of Natural History (of course); and a visit to the Statue of Liberty, where we would go right into the fingers, which is something she had always wanted to do. That was provided they let visitors in there.

Normally, whenever I offered her my ideas for fun, she

would respond by saying "great." But on this occasion, the best I could get out of her was an unenthusiastic "fine."

So I knew she had something else on her mind.

"What would you really like to do?"

"I'd tell you, but you would get angry."

"When have I ever done that?"

"Never, but you would this time."

"Try me."

She told me that what she really had her heart set on was that visit to the William Morris Agency so she could get started on movie producing. I didn't think we had a prayer of getting to see them, but I decided to humor her and looked them up in the directory. They were located in midtown somewhere between the East Side and the West Side. So we started out for their offices, taking a cab so that I could get it over with fast.

We found the building easily enough and strolled confidently into the lobby as if we had an appointment.

They had a long list of agents listed on the directory, and I picked out one of them at random. Then I told the security guard that we were from out of town and that we would like to see the agent I had picked out about movie producing. He called upstairs and to my great surprise, he told us to go right up there, the agent would try to squeeze us into his busy schedule.

At first I thought he was just being polite—but then it occurred to me that the William Morris Agency had a policy of seeing everyone who showed up—since you never knew where the idea for a great movie would come from. (Although seeing an eleven-year-old girl was pushing it a bit.)

We took the elevator up to the agent's office and introduced ourselves to the receptionist who told us to take a seat in the waiting area, and she would get us in to see the agent as soon as possible.

We joined a group of half a dozen people out there and

from the tone of their conversation, I could tell they were actors
and jugglers and the like, trying to get a break in show business.

The agent kept us waiting for half an hour or so and just as
we were about to give up on seeing him, a secretary came out
and showed us into his office.

There were two agents waiting for us in there. The older
one was a stocky individual with a ponytail and an earring and
skin that looked like old French fries. The other fellow held a
clipboard on his lap and might have been an assistant who was
just breaking into the business. Though he was far the younger
of the two, he was the one who was cleancut and conservatively
dressed and had not chosen to wear an earring and ponytail.

The senior agent took a seat in a swivel chair, puffed on a
cigar, as I had imagined all agents would, and leaned back with
his hands behind his head.

"What have you got for us?" he asked.

Since he had directed the question to me, I tried to think
of something to say, but I could not come up with anything. I
was still amazed that we had gotten in to see him at all.

Then Lettie took over and said she would like to get started
in the movie-producing business.

Before she could go any further, the senior agent cut her
off in what seemed to me like a gruff way.

"I hear you," he said, "but you can't just come in here and
expect us to hand *you* a package. We're an established agency
and you obviously don't have a track record. You've got to bring
us something."

I thought that would be the end of the interview and
frankly, I was happy we had gotten as far as we did.

What I hadn't counted on was that Lettie had come prepared for the situation.

With little hesitation, she calmly proceeded to tell him the
story of an aging firefly that was down to his last sparkle. He
hears about a little girl who is dying and decides to fly to her
bedside and do his last sparkle for her. He does—and the sick

girl is so delighted and cheered up that she recovers. And then the firefly dies.

As she told the story, the assistant agent, whose name was Ken, kept saying, "Yes . . . I hear you . . . Oh, yes . . . That's beautiful . . . I'm fainting . . . keep going."

After Lettie finished telling her story there was a silence in the room, and we all leaned in toward the senior agent to see what he would say.

He took a puff of his cigar and thought for a minute.

"Does the firefly have to die?" he asked.

"Absolutely," said Lettie.

"You'll alienate half your audience," he said. "And how can you do a sequel without the firefly? Couldn't the firefly get better?"

"That would spoil everything," said Lettie. "And who cares about a sequel."

"Who cares about a sequel," he repeated with a hoarse laugh. "Maybe that should be the title. I can see you're new in the business."

He took a reflective pull of his cigar at that point and said: "Let me think about it."

Then he instructed Ken to give Lettie a copy of a screenplay to study so she could see what a movie looked like on paper. There were at least a hundred of them on the office shelves, and after glancing at a few, Ken selected one and handed it to her.

"I was following every word of your story," he whispered to her. "And I loved it."

I figured out that the senior agent couldn't say he loved it, even if he did, but Ken could, since he wasn't putting his head on the block.

The senior agent then escorted us back to the waiting area and rang for the elevator.

"There's something there," he said, handing me a cigar. "We'll be in touch."

* * *

"THAT WAS FABULOUS," said Lettie, as we left the building.

I agreed, and if anything, I was more excited than she was. The fact that we had gotten in to see the agent was more than I had hoped for. And now he was going to give Lettie's idea some thought, which was remarkable.

For the first time, I began to take Lettie seriously as a movie producer. After all, what difference did it make how old she was? Wasn't it the quality of her ideas that counted! Maybe she would do *my* story someday, about an unemployed poultry man who gets involved in a dangerous global enterprise—and has to kill a few people. Of course, I couldn't propose it to her now. But maybe someday, when it was all behind me.

AFTER OUR MEETING with the William Morris agents, it was hard for us to get worked up about the Indians and dinosaurs on our schedule. But we went ahead and saw them anyway, since our time in New York was limited. And then we wandered back toward our apartment, stopping here and there to peek in at some of the small stores that concentrated on one type of item, such as train sets and music boxes from France.

One that intrigued us was right around the corner from our building. It supplied police equipment such as clubs and bulletproof vests to the officers and students at the nearby police academy. There were also some items available to the public, although not many.

Lettie picked out a T-shirt that said NEW YORK'S FINEST and some panties, and I selected a leather belt that didn't have much to recommend it other than that the police wore it, which was good enough for me. Somewhere along the line I had heard that wrongdoers often gravitate toward police activities. (When obviously, they should stay as far away as possible.)

If I wasn't a prime example of that phenomenon, I'd like to know who was.

Once again, we decided to turn in on the early side since Peabody was arriving the following morning and I had a big day ahead of me.

I said goodnight to Lettie and told her how proud I was of her for the way she handled herself at the William Morris Agency.

"You're the one," she said. "They wouldn't have paid any attention to me if you weren't there."

"I didn't hardly say anything."

"But you have charisma."

"If I do, I'm not aware of it. And where did you learn 'charisma'?"

"Would you like me to spell it?"

"That's all right. I'll take your word for it. And you told them an awfully good story."

"I know," she said. "I just hope they don't screw up the casting."

Chapter
Nineteen

THE NEXT MORNING, after our breakfast, I found a store nearby that sold magazines from all over the world. What I thought is that I would lay in plenty of reading material for Lettie so that she could be occupied while Peabody and I conducted our business. I assumed she would select magazines that were targeted to her age group, or at least were about the movie industry—but she picked out half a dozen fat ones that contained glossy pictures of beautiful estates in places like Mexico and the Costa del Sol. They were as expensive as entire books, but I didn't think she realized that, and I wasn't about to make it an issue. As we left the store, it occurred to me that she could read through the magazines in about twenty minutes, so I stopped in at an electronics store and bought her a Sony Walkman and some tapes, which would give her plenty to do in case I got delayed.

After making sure that Lettie was safe and sound, I went uptown to meet Peabody at some kind of gentleman's club that I assumed he belonged to. For the most part, the members were well-dressed elderly fellows who sat around in overstuffed chairs and didn't appear to have a worry in the world. It didn't take much to figure out how you got into a club like that. All you had to be was well fixed and to have the right connections.

Peabody arrived at the same time as I did, and we found a couple of overstuffed chairs of our own near the fireplace. He looked trim and well rested and was wearing an olive-colored suit that was so simple and understated that it had to have cost a lot of money.

We ordered brandies from a waiter who was old enough and distinguished-looking enough to have been a member of the club himself.

"How long have you belonged to this club?" I asked.

He took a quick look around to make sure that no one was listening.

"I'm not, actually," he said quietly. "I just pop in here now and then and no one's ever thought to question me. It *is* important to keep a pipe going, however."

"I don't have one."

"I do," he said.

With that, he produced a Sherlock Holmes–style model from his vest pocket, filled it with tobacco from a leather pouch and got it started.

"Now first off," he said, "how is your darling Lettie? Probably off dating some young ne'er-do-well, I would imagine."

"Not that I know of. She's back at the apartment, reading magazines."

"Don't you wish," he said with a laugh that was half a snuffle. "You're so innocent, Binny. She's dating her head off."

Rather than keep insisting that Lettie was not dating her head off, I decided to end that line of conversation.

"If you say so."

"The flat to your liking?" he asked.

"Couldn't be better."

"It's lovely, isn't it? Convenient location and all that. I've used it myself on occasion."

And then he got down to the matter at hand.

"There are two of them this time around, as I mentioned, and Thomas Gnu is particularly anxious to get the matter settled, which is why he's made these pukka arrangements."

"I beg your pardon."

"Pukka," he said. "Everything first-rate. You've got the apartment, he has me at the Carlyle, and I would assume the fee is satisfactory."

"It is."

"One of them, Masroor he calls himself, is a noted film producer in Karachi and the other—Gail Parsons—fancies herself as an actress. It seems that Thomas Gnu had once arranged the financing for Masroor to do a twenty-million-dollar film extolling the wonders of capitalism on the subcontinent, with Gail Parsons to star in it. Gnu quite fancied her and saw it as an opportunity to get into her knickers. At the last moment, the pair canceled the production and slipped off to do some piece of Noel Coward fluff on the stage in Peshawar. This embarrassed Gnu and has obviously stuck in his craw, making him determined once and for all to do away with them."

"What they did doesn't sound like such a heinous offense."

"Here again, you've got to know our employer. He can be quite strange at times, and of course he has enough money and power to employ fools like us to deal with his neuroses."

"Has he ever been involved in Jewish repertory theatre?" I asked, recalling the photograph that had been snipped out of the brochure.

"That's an odd question," said Peabody, who had the instincts of a snake. "Why do you ask?"

"So many people are these days."

"Indeed. That comes as news to me. But to answer your question, I can assure you that Thomas Gnu has never expressed the slightest interest in *Jewish* theater, as you put it."

He made a face when he said the word "Jewish" and I reached the obvious conclusion about his feelings toward that much-maligned people.

But I decided to let the matter drop.

"How do I get at them?"

"Easily. As it happens, Masroor is being given an award by a film society late this afternoon at the Warwind Hotel. Gail is doing the introductions, so it shouldn't present any difficulty to get at the pair of them."

For the first time, it sank in that there was a woman involved this time around, and I had to make sure that did not affect my performance. To do so, of course, would be sexist.

He handed me a badge for my lapel that said FILM SOCIETY

OF THE SUBCONTINENT and said that it would serve as my invitation.

"How would you like this done?"

"Oh yes," he said. "You've no doubt noticed a collection of antique canes and walking sticks in the foyer of the flat. There's one in particular, a tan-and-white Alaskan silkwood, quite lovely in its design. It's actually a weapon, and there's not much to it. Simply unscrew the cap at the head of it, and then it's point and shoot. It's not quite hair-trigger in its response, but the pull is light, and you shouldn't have much trouble with it. The projectile works in two stages—it feels like a mosquito bite at first and there's an eight- to ten-minute delay before it takes full effect. So there's plenty of time for you to slip away. What you might do is pretend you're bored, yawn, that sort of thing . . . the proceedings are quite dull anyway, and then you're safely off."

I recalled him saying that we would be working closely on this one, and I asked him if he would be there with me.

"I'm afraid not. Something's come up. I have to attend a meeting on some new Holocaust museum they have planned for Staten Island. Seems I volunteered to be a sponsor. Much as I looked forward to our working together in a very real sense, I'm not going to be able to manage it."

Once again, I found him to be a barrel of contradictions. He had made a face when he said *Jewish* repertory theatre, and yet here he was, showing up as the sponsor of a Holocaust memorial. At least he was consistent in his inconsistencies.

"Well then, I guess I'll have to take care of it alone."

Chapter
Twenty

FOR SOME REASON, as I walked back to the apartment to get the walking stick, the business about the photograph still nagged at me. The resemblance between the artistic director of the Jewish theatre and Thomas Gnu, as I recalled seeing him in the slide projection, was too close to be a total coincidence. And now I knew that Peabody used the apartment from time to time. Was it possible that he was the one who clipped the photograph out of the theatre brochure? And then showed it to me as a slide projection, claiming that it was Thomas Gnu? And why would he do that?

Still, this was no time to be worrying about such things. I had much more serious matters to attend to.

As I suspected, Lettie had raced through the expensive magazines featuring homes in the Costa del Sol and was now lying on the canopied bed, listening to her tapes and singing along with them. She stopped immediately when I entered the apartment, not wanting to be caught singing in front of her father.

I found the tan-and-white walking stick without difficulty and told her that I would be going out for a while.

"I thought you were just out," she said.

"I was, but I have to go out again, just this last time."

"Hold it a second," she said, taking off her earphones and vaulting down from the bed.

Then she gave me the biggest and longest hug I could remember in our time together. It was as if I was going off to war, which in a way I was.

"Just be safe," she said, during the hug.

It was as if she had sensed what I was about to do. I knew she was smart—I had seen that demonstrated in the William

231

Morris offices—but it may be that she was even smarter than I realized.

I locked her in and then strolled uptown to the Warwind Hotel, carefully tucking the walking stick under my arm so that it did not go off accidentally. But as I approached the hotel I decided I had better start using it, which I did, breaking into my limp, as though I had trouble with my hip and the walking stick was my only means of getting around.

The lobby was buzzing with activity when I got there, and unless I was mistaken, there was a faint smell of chutney in the air. Many of the people who stood around had the same ID badge as I did. Most were dark complected, the men wearing turbans and the women dressed in colorful saris. But for the most part they spoke English, the main topic of discussion being movies I had never heard of and film festivals they had just attended. Had Lettie been there, I doubt that she would have gotten much out of it, her interests being more in the area of mainstream American film fare.

After about fifteen minutes, the crowd started to drift up a flight of stairs; I limped along, following them into an auditorium, where I assumed the ceremony was to take place. Since it was of utmost importance that I get a clean and unimpeded view of the stage, I waited until most of the people had sat down and then took a seat about ten rows back and over on the extreme right aisle. It gave me the angle I was looking for and at the same time I didn't feel I was too conspicuous sitting there.

Once the crowd had settled in, a young woman came out and introduced herself as Gail Parsons, the president of the film society. She had short blonde hair, a trim and shapely body and a toothy smile that I imagine would be attractive if you liked seeing all those teeth. She said they had all gathered there to honor Masroor (he went by one name, like Cher) not for any single film he had produced but for a whole lifetime of achievement, some of it charitable. She said some other nice things about Masroor, notably his contribution to the growing film industry on the subcontinent and the helping hand he had extended to actors and actresses, herself included. Finally, she introduced the honoree himself, who came out from the wings to a huge round of applause, Gail Parsons joining in on it.

Masroor was a stocky and energetic-looking fellow with long biblical-style hair whose powerful body made him seem much taller than he was. Gail Parsons shook hands with him, gave him a hug, kicking back one shapely leg as she did so, and then walked back to take a seat on the platform.

I leaned forward to make sure I was positioned correctly and overheard a snatch of whispered conversation in the row in front of me.

"Held up quite nicely, hasn't she?"

"I'd say. She's still got the best bum in Karachi."

When I heard the second fellow's remark, I froze in my tracks as if I was the one who had been shot with the walking stick.

He had used Peabody's very words in explaining to me why he had remained tied to his wife, despite her flagrant infidelity.

I could still recall his anguished wail.

"How can I leave her, Binny? *She's got the best bum in Karachi.*"

It was a description you don't forget.

I felt as if someone had taken the bandages off my eyes, and I saw clearly that Gail Parsons was Peabody's estranged wife. And Masroor was her lover. And it was *Peabody* who wanted them killed, not Thomas Gnu. The same held true for Dickie Moué and poor Mr. Matsumoto. It was *Peabody* who'd been humiliated at Groton by Dickie Moué, *Peabody* who'd been thrown off the board by Mr. Matsumoto. For all I knew—and now I was sure of it—there *was* no Thomas Gnu. Peabody had invented him, arbitrarily using as his likeness the photograph of a fellow who was innocently heading up a Jewish repertory theatre in New Jersey.

And all this had been done to mislead me. What it meant is

that I'd been trotting around the globe, trying to settle *Peabody's* old scores, and not those of the nonexistent Thomas Gnu.

A good question is what difference did it make?

In one sense, very little. So I was working for Peabody and not Thomas Gnu. That didn't change the dollar amount I was being paid. But he had deceived me and I did not enjoy being played for a fool. How could I possibly trust him in any future endeavors? How could I trust him on this one? For all I knew I would *never* get the $250,000 and be paying interest on the advance for the rest of my life. Maybe he had arranged to have me arrested on the spot, the second I disposed of his faithless wife and her Indian lover.

Or who knows, maybe I just wasn't cut out for this type of work and was just looking for a way to get out of it.

Out of curiosity, I stayed around to listen to a little of Masroor's speech. Not that there was any way I was going to harm a hair on the man's head—or on that of Gail Parsons.

As I listened to the famed Indian filmmaker, I thought back to the start of the program, when Gail Parsons had crossed the stage to embrace him. I recalled her bum as having a decent shape to it, but as to whether it was the best Karachi had to offer I could not testify. Maybe it was the best at one time and had fallen off a bit over the years.

Masroor spoke about how honored he was to be honored by the film society and got a big laugh by saying he hoped the award wasn't a hint that he was supposed to retire.

"Rest assured," he said. "I have a lot more to say on the screen."

There was a great deal of animal magnetism to the man, and I could see why Gail Parsons might have chosen him over the quirky and in many ways passive Peabody. But under the circumstances, it was difficult for me to concentrate on the long acceptance speech. So when he got into the main body of it, which had to do with actors having to be treated like children, I stretched out a bit, yawned conspicuously and covered my mouth with an open palm.

Then I got up and prepared to make my exit.

As I did so, a fellow in the row behind me gave me a hard look.

"Rude bastard," he said under his breath.

Normally, I would not have let him get away with a remark like that, but in this instance I thought it best to keep my feelings to myself and left the auditorium without firing off a rejoinder.

As I walked back to the apartment, I felt more strongly than ever that Peabody had used me, as he had probably taken advantage of others like me. (Kevin Kurosawa would be a perfect case in point.) And who knows how many of us there were, chasing around the globe, settling his petty grievances for handsome fees we were promised and would probably never see. I only wished I could contact that poor slob in Rawalpindi and let him know what was going on.

The first thing I planned to do when I got back home was tear up that Global Enterprises coupon book. And then sit back and watch Peabody try to get the advance money back. I'd like to hear him tell me I hadn't earned it, with all the hassle I had gone through.

And I wanted to confront Peabody, too, and let him know how I felt about him, although he'd probably taken off by now and was sunning his butt in some vacation spot for the elite, like Biarritz or Portugal or some place like that.

It shows you how wrong you can be.

Chapter
Twenty-One

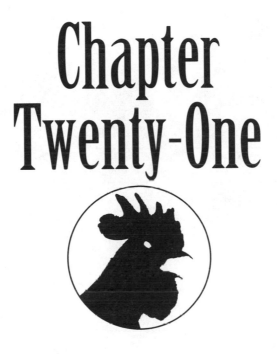

H E WAS SITTING calmly at one end of the living room couch when I unlocked the door of the apartment. Lettie was at the other end, wearing her New York City Police Department T-shirt and panties and flipping through the pages of one of the expensive magazines I had bought her. She barely looked up when I entered, but I could tell that the light had gone out of her eyes, like the firefly in her movie idea.

"Binny, dear friend," said Peabody. "That Holocaust business was over in short order so I thought I'd pop by and say hello to your daughter. How did it go at your end?"

"It didn't," I said.

And then I asked Lettie what had happened.

"Nothing," she said, not looking up from her magazine.

"I think you'd better tell me."

"You promise you won't get angry?" she said, looking up now.

"That depends."

"He wanted to smell my finger."

"There you are, old fellow," said Peabody. "All quite harmless. Certainly nothing to get into a hissy about."

I told Lettie to get dressed and to meet me at the police-equipment store. I knew she would be safe there. Then I reached into my pocket for some money and told her to pick out a few items for herself and that I would be right down to get her.

"Here now," said Peabody, reaching into his own pocket, pulling out some bills and pushing my hand aside. "Let me help out with that."

"That won't be necessary," I said.

Lettie got dressed quickly, gave me a kiss on the cheek and left the apartment.

"Lovely child," said Peabody when she was gone.

"I always thought so."

Then the phone rang and Peabody got up to take it.

"Peabody here," he said.

He listened and then covered the receiver.

"It's for your daughter."

"I'll take it."

"Lettie's not here," I told the caller. "This is William Binny, her father."

"Oh, hi. This is Ken, the assistant agent you met at the Morris office. I have some good news. We had a meeting about your daughter's idea and decided we'd like to run with it."

"Where to?"

"Where to?" he repeated, sounding puzzled. "Oh, I see. You're joking. We'd like to *option* the material for a feature film and get started on signing a writer as soon as possible. We're all thrilled with the project, and I for one knew it was a home run when I heard it. To hell with the sequel is what I feel."

"I'll let her know. And I'm sure she'll be thrilled, too."

I thanked him for the call and hung up, amazed once again at the great balance wheel of life. Something awful would happen and then, inevitably, the sun would come up. All you had to do was make sure you were around when it did.

"That sounded like good news," said Peabody.

"It was."

"May I ask what it concerned?"

"No harm in asking," I said.

And then I shot him with the walking stick. It had a light trigger pull, just as he said it would, but it did not take any eight to ten minutes for it to take effect. I had gotten him in the throat, and he did gurgle out a few words—"You've got this all wrong"—a sentiment I felt he had been a little late in expressing. But the effect was almost instantaneous.

So once again, he had deceived me.

I found some copies of Barron's financial newspaper in the

240

utility room and spread them out on the kitchen floor. Then I dragged him in there and laid him out on them. After that, I went to work with my powered Super V Turkey De-beaker, which I had felt from the start would come in handy.

I did him up in three sections, singing a little ditty to myself as a distraction.

> *I loved you Valentine Peabody*
> *How can I that deny?*
> *But you stole my daughter's inn-o-cence*
> *Therefore you had to die.*

Using double-lined garbage bags that I found in a cabinet beneath the kitchen sink, I carried the three units out to the incinerator, one by one. As luck would have it, there was nobody out there on the landing to see the operation. Then I did a complete cleanup, working primarily with chlorinated household bleach, which had also been conveniently stored beneath the kitchen sink.

After scrubbing my hands with Dial soap, I got Lettie and me packed, straightened up the apartment (which out of simple courtesy I would have done in any case) and went downstairs to meet my daughter.

I did not delude myself into thinking that I had eliminated all traces of the crime, if indeed, it *was* a crime. I was fully aware of the advances that had been made in criminal investigation, and I am not talking about DNA evidence alone, which often doesn't stand up.

As an example, they have something called electrophoretic toxicology or something like that, which can *really* put the screws to a wrongdoer. I remembered that from one of my true-crimers.

But then again, you never knew how events would unfold. Considering the way Peabody covered his tracks, renting an office, closing it up, showing up here and there, slipping around the globe like a will-o'-the-wisp, there might not be much evidence that he had ever existed. Who knows if his name was really Valentine Peabody? If I took the time to look into it, I might discover that he was really Joe Jones.

Or maybe the Karachi police would come after me and I could just about imagine how effective *they'd* be.

For the moment, I was not about to lose any sleep over making a clean getaway. I had made a reasonable effort to cover my tracks, and it would have to do. All I could think of at the moment was how calm and unruffled I had been in getting him out of the picture and the way in which several thousand years of civilization had melted away when I entered that apartment and saw my daughter's face. I was convinced that anyone in my position—except perhaps the most hardened churchgoer—would have acted the same way.

The potential is there in all of us. All you have to do is push the right button. And Peabody had certainly pushed mine.

IT OCCURRED TO me that I would have to have a few words with Ed Bivens as well. If it turned out that *he* was the one who had scouted my daughter for Peabody, I was prepared to deal with that accordingly—even going so far as to use my de-beaker, which thus far had afforded me so well.

Chapter
Twenty-Two

L ETTIE WAS EXAMINING some riot gear when I entered the police-equipment store.

"How come we're all packed?" she said.

"I finished up my work."

"But what if the William Morris Agency calls and wants to option my story?"

"They already did. You hit a homerun."

"That's amazing," she said. "And it's not even my best idea."

"You can do that one next."

"Possibly. But what do I do about school?"

"You keep going to it. And you do the producing on the side."

"I don't know if I can pull that off. I'll have to think about it."

We had an open return on our tickets and there wasn't any rush to get to the airport. So I put my arm around my daughter, and we started out on one of our great walks.

Then I got the idea of seeing a Broadway show.

"Which one should we pick?" she asked.

"Let's just go over to the Broadway area and we can decide then."

And that's what we did. The first theatre we came to was featuring *Show Boat*, which I thought would be a good choice because of its racial theme and its contribution to an under-standing of our early culture. Lettie said that although she didn't know much about the show, she was willing to give it a try. But when I went up to the box office, the ticket seller said that the evening performance was all sold out. Lettie said fine, we'd find another show that had some tickets available and might be just as good as *Show Boat*. But I could tell she was disappointed.

We bought some hot chestnuts from a vendor and then we stood outside the theatre and ate them, watching the lucky people who *did* have tickets file in. And then I spotted a little fellow in a sharkskin suit and old-fashioned spats who was shuffling tickets and mumbling as if he was talking to himself. I decided to approach him.

"What are you looking for?" he said. "I got everything. Balcony, orchestra, what do you want?"

"We'll take the best two you have," I said, "as long as they are down fudge."

"What?" he said, looking at me sharply.

I had meant to say "down front" of course, but obviously it had come out wrong. So I tried again.

"Down fudge."

"What are you, a wise guy?" he said.

Lettie took over at that point, saying I meant close to the stage, but not until she had given me a peculiar look of her own.

"I got a great pair," the fellow said, "but they'll cost you four hundred dollars."

Lettie shook her head no, but I nodded—not trusting myself to talk—and indicated that we could take them.

What the fellow didn't know is that I would have paid him a thousand dollars for them.

"Are you all right?" Lettie asked, as we entered the theatre.

"Share," I said.

"I don't think so," she said.

I had to agree with her on that—and to wonder, of course, what had happened to me. Then I realized that it had to be connected to the drama that had unfolded at the apartment on Gramercy Park. My actions in disposing of Peabody must have triggered some deep-seated justice-seeking mechanism in my brain. Ergo (that word I'd been trying to shoehorn in) the effect on my speech pattern.

I was disturbed, of course (who wouldn't be?), since speaking is tremendously important to a fellow such as myself—I hadn't realized just how important it was—and it would probably take all kinds of therapy to get me back on track. Yet in some curious way—and no matter what law enforcement was able to achieve—I was happy not to have gotten away clean.

Obviously, however, I would have preferred a more gentle slap on the wrist.

THE SEATS WERE in the tenth row center, and they were every bit as good as the scalper said they were. I had to give him that. After glancing at the program, I could judge from the number of scenes that we were in for a long evening. I wasn't sure I could tolerate all that entertainment in one sitting, as upset as I was. But once the show started, I got caught up in it and forgot about how long it was going to be.

Just watching the scenery alone made me feel we had gotten our money's worth. I recognized most of the music, but it was all new to my daughter, and to tell the truth, I spent most of the time watching Lettie watch the show and seeing the light come back into her eyes.

The high point of the first act came when a big burly black fellow came out and sang, "Old Man River" in a voice as deep and rich as the Mississippi itself. The audience went wild when he finished singing it. The show continued, of course, but from time to time, they would bring the same fellow back to sing a few bars of the same song. The audience was glad to see him, but each time he came out on stage, their applause was a little less enthusiastic. It soon became clear that the only reason they were bringing him out was so that you wouldn't notice they were

changing the scenery. I thought that was a mistake and considered asking Lettie about it, but I didn't want it to come out
wrong. And more important, I didn't want to interfere with her
enjoyment of the show. So I didn't say anything to her, although
I was confident that as an up-and-coming producer, she would
agree with me.

IT HAD BEEN quite a trip. The great apartment in Gramercy Park,
the dinosaurs and restaurants, Lettie's movie deal, the whole
Peabody business—you name it—and then getting to see a
Broadway musical comedy in seats that were so close to the stage
we might as well have been right up there with the actors. I did
not see how we could possibly squeeze in any more excitement—but try telling that to Lettie who was just getting warmed
up.

"Let's do something else," she said, when the show was
finally over and the audience had stopped applauding.

"If you can think of something."

"I can," said Lettie. "What about a horse-and-buggy ride
through Central Park. I've dreamed of taking one ever since I
was a little girl."

"I hadn't realized that," I said, unaware that she had
crossed over into maturity—which, as far as I was concerned,
she hadn't. (They could make her the head of a Hollywood
studio and I would feel the same way.)

The other shows had emptied out by the time we got to the
street, causing us to get caught up in a huge, slow-moving crowd
of theatregoers. They seemed in no hurry to get home, which
was fine with me, considering the day I had put in. But Lettie
suddenly ducked her head down, grabbed my hand and started
to fly through the crowd, pulling me along behind her like
some kind of kite she was trying to get off the ground. I held on
and had to laugh at the spectacle—an eleven-year-old string-

bean hauling a fully grown man behind her (and don't forget my suitcase). Where did she get that kind of strength, I wondered? Could it have been the twelve ballet lessons I had invested in? If so, they had certainly begun to pay off.

She whipped and zigzagged us up to the edge of Central Park South and we didn't stop to catch our breath until we had signed on for one of the fabled buggy rides. The horse we got was a little on the old side but had remained proud and regal all the same. And our buggy was fit for a king. Lettie insisted that we put blankets over our legs, even though I was doing fine without them.

"No, no," she said. "It's part of it."

Then we settled in to enjoy the clip-clop of the horse's hooves, the mysterious park and the stately buildings that surrounded it. From what we could see, each of the apartments was warmly lit and had a romantic feel to it. We wondered about the people who lived in them. They couldn't all be Faye Dunaway. So who were they? Or at least *I* wondered about these things. Even though she had been dreaming about it for years, Lettie quickly lost interest in the whole operation.

"Would you give me one of your famous head massages?" she asked.

"In a *buggy*?" I said, acting more startled than I was. "And since when did they become famous?"

"Are you *kidding*!" she said. "They're fabulous."

She had not quite answered my question, but when she snuggled up against my shoulder, I gave her one of the famous head massages anyway. I would come in with one now and then—at home—when my wizard's imaginary sleep dust didn't work.

She fell asleep immediately, making me the only one there to enjoy the ride that she had been so desperate to take.

But there were certain advantages to the situation. For one thing, my speech was still a little shaky and I was concerned about my ability to handle certain words, chief among them my favorite in the whole English language. So I thought I might as well use the opportunity to try it out. Keeping my voice low so as not to disturb either Lettie or the driver, I whispered it in the darkness—*daughter*—and was delighted when it came out clear as a bell.